Cemetery Street

Cemetery Street

BRENDA SEABROOKE

Holiday House / *New York*

For Kevin and Kerria,
with thanks
to Julie and Mary C.

Library of Congress Cataloging-in-Publication Data
Seabrooke, Brenda
Cemetery Street / by Brenda Seabrooke.—1st ed.
p.   cm.
Summary: Courtney Carmichael, her younger brother,
and her depressed, newly-divorced, out-of-work mother
move from New Hampshire to Florida into a decrepit
house on Cemetery Street, where spooky occurrences
make the family feel increasingly unsettled.
ISBN 978-0-8234-2115-2 (hardcover)
[1. Family problems—Fiction.   2. Supernatural—
Fiction.   3. Florida—Fiction.]   I. Title.
PZ7.S4376Ce 2008
[Fic]—dc22
2008013653

Prologue

Dark nothingness pushes against me like the inside of the worst nightmare you've ever had, the kind that threatens your life, your soul. I open my mouth to scream, but, like in a nightmare, no sound comes out. Darkness rushes inside me, filling me up until breathing is hard and I take tiny little breaths, afraid each one will be my last. I've fallen into that dread black hole everyone fears because it is the opposite of life.

I can see nothing, not even my fingers in front of my face. Blackness surrounds me, cloying, like a dusty black curtain, thick as velvet, that sticks to me as I breathe in the suffocating folds. I reach out and touch something. A shelf. I feel around. My hands define a long boxlike shape. The surface is cold and hard. Metal. A box. Long. Metal. A CASKET!

Help! Somebody help me!

No one does. No one can hear me. I am in a tomb,

and the walls absorb all sound and light and life. This is a house for the dead. I flail around blindly, and my fingertips graze more shelves, more caskets, wooden coffins. How many are in here? I don't know. I don't want to know. It smells like death. Musty, dank, hideous death. I think I can smell decaying bodies.

I stand in the center of the tomb and wrap my arms around me, afraid that I'll touch a bone or a mummy. I'm shaking and can't stop. How long have I been in here? I try the door but it's solid, locked. How long can a person live locked in a tomb? I try to remember stories I've read about people entombed after earthquakes, mudslides, people fallen into wells. I can't think of a single one where a person has been locked in a tomb except maybe in an Edgar Allen Poe story. That's not a comforting thought. All his stuff is so creepy, and it usually ends badly for somebody. In this case, the somebody is me. I don't want to end badly. I don't want to end. Not yet. Not for a long time. I haven't got my driver's license yet. Nobody in the world knows this, but I haven't been kissed yet either.

This is a dream. It has to be a dream. Any minute I'll wake up and see the walls of my room, the palm trees and jabbering parrots outside the window. I'll hear Bucky snoring in his bed. Mom will be doing one of her silly projects. I'll wake up safe in my room. My room on Cemetery Street.

Chapter 1

The car finally died on Limbo Key. It had sputtered all along the roller-coaster trip from New Hampshire. We were headed as far south as you can go in the continental USA, but I guess it was fate that picked this place for the car's demise.

"See if you can find what's wrong, Courtney," Mom said.

How many times had I heard that? Mom always thinks I can do whatever she can't, especially if it's mechanical. As if I knew anything about cars. I unhitched my seat belt and got out of the Honda circa 1776. Mom popped the hood. The metal was hot, searing my fingers. Not surprising—the September sun had poured down on us since we'd left Georgia sometime before dawn this morning. I sucked my smarting fingers and gave Mom a look. She didn't even notice. Her attention was on something beyond me. I think my mom has had ADD since her last divorce.

I sighed and used the end of my T-shirt to open the hood. Clouds of steam whooshed up. Instant facial. Or sunburn. I stepped back until the steam cleared. The car's engine looked like the burned-out lab of some mad scientist.

"I don't see anything," I said, meaning anything I could fix. Mom wasn't listening. Horns blared behind us. We were backing up traffic all the way to Miami, judging by the decibels.

"Push the car while I steer it over there." Mom pointed at the parking area in front of a building beside the road.

I ignored the angry looks and horn symphony as I gave the Honda a shove.

"Look, Courtney." Mom shaded her eyes, which were hidden by rhinestone-framed sunglasses. "Head over there. It's a realty office. Maybe it's a sign. We can just stay here. After all, when you don't have a place to go to, any place will do."

I didn't think that was right. We'd left New Hampshire headed for a specific place where Mom could do her art thing—Key West. How did she know this island would do? Maybe people on Limbo Key hated art. Maybe they ran artists out of town on a rail. Maybe they taxed artists and made them get licenses. I could find a lot of reasons why Limbo Key might not be a good place. I could probably even find some based on what I could see of it from where I stood. Hot. Tinselly. No mall.

And I didn't like the name. Who wants to live in a place with a name that means the middle of nowhere? I mean, it's not heaven or earth. How can you get your feet on the ground on an island in limbo? Maybe it's not really an island. Maybe it floats. Like we do. First, my mom and me and whatever husband she had, then Bucky too. And Bucky's dad, and then her last husband, if he ever was her husband. I think my mom has been married five times. I'm not really sure. Some of those "husbands" may have been just boyfriends. She said they were married, but I don't remember any divorces when they left. She needed to be more discerning in her choices. None of them were dope dealers, but they weren't choirboys either. Bucky's dad was probably the best of the lot.

In New Hampshire and Maine and once in Vermont when I was really little, the land under our feet had been rock solid—all those mountains, and everybody knows mountains stay in one place. They don't float or wash away like sandy islands. Maybe it wouldn't be good for Mom to live on an island. Maybe she needed those mountains to anchor her. Since we left New England, she seemed floatier than usual.

The highway ran along the eastern edge of Limbo Key. Across the road behind bait shops and boat rentals, the green water of the ocean sparkled like a zillion diamonds. Right now I didn't blame Mom for her escapist fantasies. I felt like running across the street, jumping in, and swimming away myself.

"You're not pushing, Courtney," Mom said.

I hadn't stopped, but the Honda wasn't moving an inch. A high, nervous horn beeped above the others. I turned and gave the horn blower behind me a look that should have shut him up. You'd think he could get out and help. We weren't blocking traffic on purpose. Where was male chivalry when you really needed it? Or common sense?

I made Bucky get out so the car would weigh about a ton less. Mom had to push from the driver's side before we could budge it. We finally rolled the Honda onto the edge of the parking lot in front of a strip of shops. The horns stopped as traffic resumed except for one long blast as a gold Lexus sped by. I refrained from making any sort of gesture.

"Stay with your brother," Mom said and went in the realty office.

Bucky and I sat on a rock in the shade of a spindly palm, dislodging lizardy things that ran for their lives. A rumor of a breeze flitted by. Bucky was intent on some battle between anthropomorphic machinery and giant mutant insects. I don't know how he can figure out who the good guys are. Bucky's father keeps him supplied with games, so he doesn't have to have him over for visits. It suits everybody but me. I have to baby-sit Buchanan Elroy Bannister III.

When the last husband took off, Mom took a class where you looked into yourself to find the you there. Then she read a book that said artists had trouble fitting into society. She decided since she had trouble doing just that, she must be an artist. She started making these little crafty things—dolls out of clothespins. They took a long time to make and didn't bring in much money. So she moved on to painting rocks and then pieces of old wood she found, and then to watercolors and finally to canvas. She didn't make much money from her art, maybe because her paintings were desolate barn scenes or sad-looking mountains, dreary trees, and mournful clouds. I didn't know you could make mountains and barns and trees look sad, but Mom was pretty good at it. She had high hopes for her new career even though she'd never had any training.

"You don't need training to paint what's inside you," she said. "Anyway I've had some training. I decorated the bulletin boards all the time when I was in school, and I always made the Valentine box. That was so much fun."

I wasn't totally against her new career. It beat having her quitting jobs all the time just before getting fired for daydreaming or making mistakes. She was always terrified of getting fired, because she said it made it harder to get jobs. These were all jobs that didn't come attached to unemployment for some reason.

Mom is really pretty and she tries, but she doesn't seem able to concentrate and she's been sad for a long time. Losing husbands is bound to get to you. We lived off Bucky's dad's checks, which were barely enough for Bucky and way not enough for the three of us. Mom doesn't get any checks for me. My dad was a soldier or maybe a sailor or Marine she met one weekend on a trip to Atlantic City with girlfriends when she was 16. They didn't have time to get married before he shipped out. He was killed, she said, somewhere in the Mideast. Maybe that's why she gets married all the time, because she didn't the first time. Once I suggested that maybe I should get something from the army, but it turned out she didn't even know his right name.

Mom didn't finish high school and doesn't have any confidence in her abilities—except the artistic talent she says she was born with. She has way too much confidence in that, but, who knows, maybe sunshine will cheer her up and her paintings will start selling.

Mom wasn't in the office long. She came out with

her mouth clamped in a tight line and the freckles standing out on her pale face.

Bucky looked up from his game. "Uh oh."

"In the car, kids."

"What happened?"

"Everything is too expensive here."

"You mean nothing is available to rent for less than ten dollars?" I couldn't resist.

"Don't be a smart alice."

"I'm not. That's what you said you had left after you got the new used tires put on in North Carolina." We'd left a trail of car parts all the way down I 95.

"There must be a rental somewhere we can afford," she said. "Get in the car and we'll look for some that aren't listed with an agency."

Bucky and I didn't move.

"Come *on.*" Mom opened her door. It groaned on its hinges.

"Aren't you forgetting something?" I said.

She pushed up her sunglasses. Her green eyes had this unfocused look. "What?"

"Car's dead."

"It was probably just overheated." She got in, and Bucky and I followed reluctantly. She slammed the door so hard I thought it would fall off next.

"Seat belts." She snapped hers and stuck the key in

the ignition. The car started up as if it were about to be driven off the showroom floor at some posh dealership.

"See? I told you. It's another sign." I didn't remind her that the realty office hadn't worked out, and that was surely a sign of something not good like maybe the island was already rejecting us. Mom was elated. In her world, something had gone right today.

She turned west down the street that ran alongside the realty office. "Look for rental signs in windows," she said, fluttering a hand out the window.

I picked up the map she had brought from the realtor's and tried to find the street we were on. Limbo Key looked fairly big as islands go. The houses on Hibiscus Street were stuccoed in pastels. Lots of statuary but no flamingos tucked away in the jungly plantings. On Hinton Street, the houses were older, two-storied, wooden, with wide porches. Now and then, we passed bigger houses that looked like ships. Trees with shiny bulbous trunks and limbs lined the roads. Huge oaks spread their branches in wide hugs and dark green piney things waved in the soft island breeze. "See, even the trees are welcoming," Mom said with a grin.

We turned off Jones Street and kept turning. "Do you know where you're going?"

"No. I'm just following my instincts. I believe in karma. My karma will guide us."

I refrained from saying her karma had brought us to a place where we didn't know anybody, in a car on its last wheels. And we had almost no money. Really great karma.

Bucky flopped around in the backseat. I leaned back and squinted at the relentless sun. No wonder Gauguin painted purple shadows and red horses in Tahiti. Light could do strange things to your perception. I wondered if Mom had lived in Florida in a previous life. Or maybe Tahiti. Maybe she knew Gauguin. I didn't say this out loud. I didn't want to encourage her. Next she would say that Gauguin had taught her how to paint. Or asked her to marry him.

The houses shrank in size as we drove along. Now they were mostly one-story cottages. Old cars or boats cluttered yards, along with faded flamingos and gnomes painted in primary colors. Why couldn't the gnomes fade and the flamingos stay bright pink? Hammocks swung from trees, and at least three were occupied.

"The agent told me that Limbo Key is a great place for artists." Mom began chattering. It meant she was feeling insecure. I hoped she didn't stop to ask directions from some guy and then marry him.

"They have art galleries and shows here all the time. I can just feel that this is where we're meant to be."

"Was that before or after the agent found out you can't afford to live here?"

"I don't think I like your tone, young lady. Don't be a . . ."

"I know. A smart alice."

"Mom, can I have a dog?" Bucky took this moment to put in his usual request.

"I don't see any reason why you can't, after we get settled," Mom said.

We didn't even have a place to sleep tonight, and already Mom had us living a cozy greeting-card life, a little cottagey place with light shining out of quaint multi-paned windows, dog on the hearth, cat in a rocking chair.

"I don't think that's such a good idea," I began as Mom wrenched the wheel and made a left turn. "Wait! Don't turn here, Mom!"

"Why not? I see a sign." She pointed at a cardboard sign tied around a palm trunk.

"Because it's Cemetery Street."

"Where did you see that?"

"On the street sign at the corner. And here." I flapped the map at her.

"Don't be silly." Mom tossed her bangs. "Who would name a street Cemetery Street? Repose Lane or Heavenly Close would be more appropriate."

"You should be in advertising. This is definitely Cemetery Street, and we definitely don't want to live here." I had to keep her going forward. Mom was good at turning onto wrong roads. Once we were driving south to Brattleboro, Vermont, and ended up in Canada. "That's impossible," she said when I told her. "Those signs aren't in Canadian." I don't know if she was joking.

By the map, we were in the dead center of the island. On the left, a tangled jungle grew all the way to the curb. On the right, a six-foot wall of stuccoed bricks blocked the view. I could guess what was on the other side. No streets intersected Cemetery, but, after a three-block length, the wall opened with an iron arch that had Limbo Island Cemetery spelled out across the top in scrolley iron letters. At the end of the street, a hand-lettered sign in red FOR SALE OR RENT hung from a post on the saggy porch of a wooden cottage set in jungle. It looked empty and neglected. The porch slumped to the right as if it had had a stroke. My stomach slid lower than the porch. I didn't want to live in a house at the end of Cemetery Street. Had our lives come to a dead end?

"It's so quiet here," Mom rhapsodized.

Quiet? Things screamed, slithered, and rattled in the jungle around us. Something squawked in a tree. In contrast, the other side of the wall was as silent as a tomb.

Chapter 2

We followed the sign's directions up a shell track in the jungle on the other side of the road where the owner of the cottage lived in an old two-story wooden house with boats and cars in the yard. I didn't spot any gnomes or flamingos. At the sound of our car, a man rolled out of a hammock and sauntered over. He had thick gray hair and a deep tan and looked a bit like a teddy bear in a too-small T-shirt, paint-spattered shorts, and flip-flops. I could tell by the way Mom was twinkling that she thought he was cute.

"Here we go again," I said to Bucky, as we drove away with the key.

"Don't be a smar—"

"I know. A smart alice."

"Can I have a dog?" Bucky asked again. It was the sort of punctuation he liked to add to conversations. A lot.

"Mr. Gower is probably a happily married man," Mom said.

Yeah. Like what woman would put up with living in that place? I didn't say it out loud. I didn't want Mom to answer. She might volunteer.

So we moved in. The cottage had once been the caretaker's quarters for the cemetery, but nobody wanted to live and work so close to graves anymore so Mr. Gower had bought it. Mom paid him the first month's rent. For some reason, he didn't ask for the last month's rent or a security deposit. Probably because the cottage was so beat up, with loose floorboards, floppy screens, and scarred walls. Turned out Mom had a little more than ten dollars with her, but we didn't have any furniture (and not many clothes either) so we would have to do some serious scrounging. The cottage was surprisingly clean inside, and we could use our sleeping bags the first night. It wasn't very comfortable on the hard floor, but it beat sleeping in the car.

Mom insisted that we each stay in our own rooms. "Just pretend it's all furnished and everything," she chirped. "Here's your bed, Bucky, and your chest is over here, and I think we'll put a bookcase here and a toy box here and how about a desk?"

Bucky got into the spirit of the thing, choosing a corner for a dog bed. For a while things seemed almost normal. I was happy to have a room to myself. Mom snores sometimes and Bucky makes a little blippety sound, but of course I never do.

I lay on top of my sleeping bag and looked at the strange lights that flashed on my ceiling. I felt strange. This island was so far from anything I had ever known with its constant chorus of tree frogs and insects. I expected Indiana Jones to show up any minute.

Suddenly a shape hovered in the doorway. It wasn't Indiana Jones. Or even Tarzan. Too small. A little ghost? A fugitive from across the street?

"Coco?" it whispered. It was Bucky.

"What?" I whispered back.

"Did you see something?"

"Like what?"

"Something." He paused for a minute then blurted, "Something scary."

"Yes," I said. "I see a little boy ghost carrying a sleeping bag."

After a second he giggled. "Aw, I mean really."

"No."

"Did you hear something?"

I waited.

Then he said, "I did. I saw something. And I heard something too."

I didn't ask what. Bucky had a vivid imagination. Got that from Mom. He told me anyway. "I saw a scary mean face, and it went whoooooo."

"Okay, Buckets. You can stay in here tonight. But

only tonight. Sometimes things look scarier in the dark. Just try to picture how they look in the daylight. Then you won't be scared."

I didn't tell him I'd seen strange lights across the street. I'd hung a bathrobe over one of my windows and an old pillowcase over the other to make sure I didn't see anything out there. And that nothing out there saw me. I didn't look across the street at night. What you don't see can't scare you. Much.

Bucky unrolled his sleeping bag, and I was soon treated to the delightful putt putt of his motor. It was surprisingly comforting.

The next day we got mattresses at Goodwill and brought them home on the top of the car with Bucky and me leaning out a window on each side holding them up. Mom drove real slow, so everybody on Limbo Key got a good look at us.

I picked up a stack of fashion magazines put out at the curb for recycling. They were pretty old, but it was something to read. And they doubled as a nightstand, though I didn't have a lamp to put on it, just my beat-up Mickey Mouse clock. The only light in my room came from a naked bulb hanging from a cord.

We found an old love seat at the curb too and brought that home hanging out of the trunk. I had to walk along behind to keep it from falling out. I didn't really mind scrounging for stuff as long as nobody saw us, but Mom didn't seem to want to go out at night.

We dragged the love seat into the living room and threw a sheet over it to cover where the stuffing was coming out. Presto! Our living room was furnished. The kitchen table was a packing crate with palm stumps for stools. We also used palm stumps for end tables. They are so versatile. People leave them out for curbside pickup all cut in nice lengths that can be stacked. Our kitchen decor included plastic dishes and forks saved from fast food restaurants.

I waited for Mom to look for more furniture, but she didn't. She just wandered around in her ratty old bathrobe or played solitaire with a pack of ratty old cards she kept in her ratty old pocket. Her eyes had a sort of dazed look as if she had got us this far and couldn't go any farther. We ate the remains of our trip food, heavy on the cheese crackers. Actually, hot dogs simmered in grape jelly with pickle relish aren't too bad. The jelly came in little packets from the breakfast bar in the one motel we stayed in on the trip down.

After three days I took stock. This was worse than camping. At least when you're camping you have the cozy campfire to huddle around. And hot dogs and marshmallows to roast on sticks. We only had mattresses on the floor. No more hot dogs. No marshmallows.

"Mom, we need to get groceries. We can stop at some yard sales on the way."

She looked up from her cards, spread out on the packing crate. "How do we know there are any yard sales to go to?"

What was wrong with her? "It's Saturday morning, Mom. All over the continental United States there are yard sales, except maybe in California where it's only"—I thought quickly—"six A.M."

"Maybe later. I'm too tired right now." She laid out a fresh game, slapping the cards on the crate.

"Mom, how can you be tired? I realize that solitaire takes a lot of energy, but you just got up." And you haven't done anything for days. I didn't say that. Today I was a selective smart alice.

"I know, but I just can't seem to get enough sleep. That trip was tiring." For emphasis, she yawned. She forgot to mention smart alice. That was worrying. She'd never been too tired to remind me of my manners before.

I had to be firm with her. "Mom, we need furniture. We can't live on the floor like dogs."

Bucky's ears pricked at the magic word. "Mom, can I—"

"No," I cut him off. "Mom, come on, let's go to some yard sales."

"I told you, I don't have money to spend on anything but food now."

"Let's go see what's in the free boxes," I urged. "At least we can do that."

"How do we know where to go?"

Had she left her brains in New Hampshire? "Mom, all we have to do is drive up and down the streets where there are houses—you know where people live—and . . ."

"Don't be a smart alice."

For once I didn't mind her saying that. She sounded more like her old self. I was relieved when she pulled on a pair of old jeans and a faded red T-shirt. We piled in the car.

"Can I get a dog?" Bucky said as she fired up the engine, and I didn't mind him saying that because it sounded normal too.

Bucky found some old books in one free box, and I found a dented pot and mismatched lid in another and some raggedy pot holders, a 1980 dictionary, *Far from the Madding Crowd* with a torn paperback cover, several glasses, and some aluminum pie plates in another. As I cleaned out yet another free box, a woman frowned at me. Was there a law against taking everything in a free box? Did yard sales have laws I didn't know about? I smiled sweetly at her and said, "The orphans will appreciate having their own towels."

She looked confused, probably trying to remember if there were any orphanages around Limbo Key. Okay, I was being an S.A. (smart alice), but it was deliberate. I felt all prickly inside, like I was stealing from orphans instead of helping the yard sellers by carting off some of their junk. We needed that junk. That woman probably had plenty of towels. She didn't need these thin unraveling things that most people would use for dust rags. I waited at the car with Bucky, but Mom was taking a long time. When I went to see what was keeping her, she was buying a pack of cards. For five dollars.

I lost it. I grabbed her arm as she paid for the cards. "Mom, you have cards. You don't need any more."

"I don't have any like these. These are tarot cards. Never been out of the box." She showed me the unbroken seal.

"Mom, you can get some later somewhere else. We need that money for food." I kept my voice down, but the man with a money belt around his waist heard and gave me a sharp look. Maybe he thought it was an act to try to get him to lower the price.

"That's as low as I can go on the cards, ma'am. They belonged to my wife's cousin, and she put ten dollars on them so you're already getting a bargain."

I gave him the sweet smile treatment and tried to get

Mom to put them back, but the money was already in the man's belt and she was pulling me toward the car.

I was seething. This wasn't mom behavior. She was supposed to be looking after us. Making a nest for her nestlings. That quaint cottagey thing. "We could've bought something more useful with that five dollars," I said, eyeing the strange picture on the cover of the box. "Like food, for example."

"Don't be a smart alice."

"I'm not," I protested. "Our cupboard is bare."

"Have you gone to bed hungry a single night in your life?" she asked, opening the car door, her green eyes flashing.

I didn't answer. I could remember nights when all we had was a handful of dry cereal because she'd forgotten to go to the store. Or maybe she forgot because she didn't have any money. My mother didn't always tell me everything. I had to try to figure it out for myself, piece together clues. I was willing to cut her some slack about those times. Maybe she said she forgot so we wouldn't be scared at having nothing else to eat. I also didn't remind her about lunchless days at school because we didn't have any food in the house or money for me to buy lunch. Mom didn't like to dwell on the past. She preferred to hope for a magic future, one that usually involved Prince Charming.

We went to the grocery store, and she bought a bag

of dried beans, a bag of rice, an onion, and milk. It was bland food, one step up from gruel. We would have to season with the picnic packets, but at least we probably wouldn't starve. Not yet.

Going out seemed to energize Mom a little. She found an abandoned picnic table on her own and wrestled a tombstone she found in the backyard into the living room to use as a coffee table. Bucky and I came back from a walk and found it in front of the sofa. It must've been rejected by the cemetery. Then I had another thought. Somebody must have helped her move it. She couldn't have done it by herself. She just laughed when I asked who.

"I have powers," she said, giving me a mysterious look.

"Uh huh." I refrained from saying if you have powers, why didn't you conjure us up a roast or chicken instead of beans and rice? Why a tombstone, which none of us needed, we hoped, for a long time?

Bucky and I avoided that macabre table, but Mom put her coffee cups on it and propped her feet on it and laid out her cards on it. The tombstone had had writing on it, but time had weathered the letters so they were unreadable now. At least she hadn't propped it up on palm stumps to use for a kitchen table. Eating off tombstones, even an unused one, was just too creepy.

With a place to live and some furniture, Mom was

somewhat rejuvenated. School was next on the agenda. She insisted on driving us. Monday morning she herded us into the car to take Bucky to Limbo Middle School, but he threw up before we had cleared the driveway. I recognized the sounds and yelled for Mom to stop, at the same time opening the door and shoving him out just as he barfed on the crunchy coral rook driveway. He stood up. "Can I get a dog?"

We cleaned him up and dropped him at school. I thought she should go in with him, but she said he knew what to do. It wasn't like we had never moved to a new school. We knew the drill.

Then it was my turn to be that dreaded creature, the NEW KID. I've been in 14 schools. That's almost a school for every year I've been alive. I'm counting pre-school, of course, but still 14. It's probably a record.

Mom urged that old Honda right up in front of Limbo Key High School, arriving just as buses offloaded kids and groups left their cars in a parking lot. They all headed for the front of the school straight toward the Honda. It was like I had an audience. I never liked being noticed at school. Now I had no choice.

I unclenched my stomach, opened the door, and, with my chin up, I stepped out, my right foot landing smack into a steaming pile of fresh squishy dog poo.

Chapter 3

Stereophonic laughter reverberated off the walls of the school, buses, cars, palm trees. Even the parrots must have been falling off their perches laughing. That warm stuff oozing around the sides of my sandal made me feel like throwing up—but not here in front of the school. I kicked off my sandal and hopped around, wiping my foot on the grass in a sort of weird dance, saying, "Eeuw eeuw eeuw" with each hop.

"Close the door, Courtney," Mom said, eager to be off. I slunk back on the seat and told her to take me home. I left the ruined sandal on the curb.

"You have to go to school, young lady."

I let the aroma of my foot answer for me.

She wrinkled her nose. "What is that smell?"

I held up my foot. Even after wiping it on the grass, the brown stain was highly visible. And smellable.

She fired up the engine and took me home pronto, cornering on two wheels.

By the time I had scrubbed my foot, put on flip-flops, and got back to school, first period was almost over. I didn't care. I had changed my jeans for shorter pants and my blue T-shirt for a red one. I was taking no chances. I even changed earrings and pulled my hair into a ponytail. Maybe nobody would recognize me. After a stint being official in the office, I slid into a seat in second period French. I managed to stay incognito in French, but not in my next class, biology. I heard the titters and hoped they weren't about me, but of course they were. I was the star of the school for the rest of the day. Soon a rhyme circulated around the halls. Courtney who? That new girl, the one who stepped in doggie poo. Eeuw eeuw eeuw. When people saw me in the halls, they broke into the Doggy Poo Stomp, which involved a lot of foot-waving and nose-holding and eeuw eeuw eeuwing.

Things got worse. Somehow, somebody discovered where I lived, and by seventh period I was Courtney Carmichael, the girl from Cemetery Street. They trotted out their puerile graveyard jokes.

"The last thing in home addressees."

"Knock knock. Who's there? Ghoul. Ghoul who? Ghoul morning."

Lots of do do do do dooooos.

I ignored it all and tried to keep my head up, but it was hard. The next day somebody put plastic poo on my seat in lab. I sat on it anyway and took it with me when I left. Whoever did it was out the cost of fake dog poo. Anyway, I might find a use for it. Or I could sell it at a yard sale next time we moved.

I needed to get control. But how?

I did what I've always done at a new school. I wrapped myself in an imaginary parka, head to toe, and sailed through the halls on an imaginary ice floe. It was protection of some sort, and the ragging dwindled a bit. I didn't make eye contact with anybody and by Friday, when the girl who had the locker next to mine peered around the door, I was surprised. "Hi!" I said, trying out a smile.

"I wanted to see if you had any ghosts in there," she said, straight-faced. "In case they followed you to school. Or pooped in there."

I wanted to smack her. I also wanted to smack myself for being so gullible. I focused on her locker. She had covered the inside of the door in blue-and-white dotted paper and hung a mirror with frilly white tieback window curtains so that when she looked in the mirror she would see herself looking in the window.

"Cute."

"Thanks." She thought I meant it. I was being sarcastic, but it *was* clever in a cottagey sort of way. She sort of smiled at me as she turned to go. Did that make us sort of friends? I didn't even know her name.

I only knew Josh, the boy assigned to me as a lab partner in biology. He'd come in late too, but he had a better reason. He had been crewing a yacht down from Connecticut. His father probably owned the marina or the yacht club. Anyway something rich. He was tall and tan and easy on the one eye I allotted to him as he slid onto the next stool. His hair was a lighter brown than mine and had blond streaks. I wondered if they were real. If they were, would I get them? I hoped so. They really highlighted his face. If they weren't real, did I seriously want to know a boy who streaked his hair? I would have to think about that one. But not much.

On Friday, the Limbo High *Gumbo* came out. I picked up a copy on the way to lab and scanned it as I walked, hoping I wasn't in it. In a column cleverly called "The Bloggo," an item read:

Will the new girl start a fad for flip-flops in school? *Bloggo* does not recommend brown "mud" baths as a beauty aid for your feet. And what's with the new dance craze in the halls, the Doggy Poo Stomp?

"Cute."

I didn't know I had spoken aloud until Josh said, "What?"

I looked up to see two mega blue eyes looking at me. Say something clever. I couldn't think of anything. "Um, very clever writing."

"We think so," he said with a pleasant smile.

We got to our station and perched on my stool was another of those plastic dog poos.

"What's this?" Josh asked.

"Just something that seems to follow me around. Maybe it's a Buffy thing." I took out a tissue, picked it up, wrapped it up with previous poo, fished a ponytail ribbon out of my purse and secured the wrapping, tying it like a present with a bow. Josh watched me without comment. I dropped it into my purse and opened the lab manual.

After school, Josh caught up with me outside and fell into step.

"What, no sports car? No limo? No Harley?"

"Sorry about the flip-flop thing," he said to my surprise. "I didn't know it was you when I okayed the item."

"You okayed it?" I raised an eyebrow. I had practiced a lot and was good at it.

"Hey, you're good at that," he said. "Did it take you long?"

I started to say I was born with talent but decided that working for it showed I had character. "Three months one summer."

He laughed. "I'm sophomore associate editor. You seem fairly articulate. Why don't you join the staff?"

Was he serious? "Would there be an initiation?"

"No, but if there was, you've already had yours."

"I don't know. I've never been all that great at writing." Actually I'd won an essay contest on the radio for Mother's Day when I was ten, a gift certificate from Doris's Beauty Bob. I think Mom got a pedicure.

"You should give it a try. It's fun and comes with a future. From print journalism it's just a step to TV, though some think that's a step backward. The school is planning an in-house TV station after the first of the year, if you're interested."

"I'll think about it."

He nodded and walked on a few steps. "So where are you from?"

I considered. Which state was I mostly from? "Upper New England, but I've moved around a lot."

"Yeah? Me, too. My parents were and are in the military. I know what it's like to be the dreaded new kid in school." He laughed. I did too, but I bet he thought it was about as funny as I did.

"What do you mean are and were in the military?"

"My dad's retired. My mom is deployed."

It sounded like *his* home life was in limbo too.

All was going well until we reached Cemetery Street.

"This is where you live?" I could see one of his eyebrows struggling to rise, but it couldn't make it, and both went up. It was almost as cute as the sideways thing.

"Yes. Drop by sometime. We sit on the front porch every afternoon sipping iced tea and watching the grass grow on the graves. See ya."

"Yeah."

Cemetery Street didn't have a sidewalk, so I had to walk on the edge of the pavement unless I wanted to risk snakebite on the jungle side or hug the cemetery wall on the other. Since there was hardly any traffic, I walked down the middle of the narrow street. I stopped to check the mailbox to see if Bucky's check had come. It was possible. Maybe. Nah—what was I thinking? This was the U.S. postal service. No way a letter could get here this quickly.

I took out a sheaf of flyers. Automotive coupons. A dry cleaner's ad. Special shrimp night at the Bait Shack. A red flyer with bold black writing caught my eye. DEVIL WORSHIP! HERE IN YOUR OWN TOWN! COME TO A LECTURE FRIDAY NIGHT BY FORMER FBI PSYCHOLOGIST AND DEVIL-WORSHIP EXPERT DR. GABRIEL WHITE AT THE LIMBO LIBRARY—8 P.M.

Two pictures illustrated the flyer, one of a tomb desecrated with what must be signs of the devil and another of a girl with blood dripping from her mouth.

I shoved all the mail into the recycling bag on the screened back porch and unlocked the door. The fridge was in its usual basically bare mode. I hoped Mom was stopping off at the store on the way home with Bucky. I hoped she had some money left. Meanwhile I nibbled a stick of celery she had forgotten to put in his lunch. I drank a glass of water and with nothing else to do—no TV, no radio—decided to walk over to the cemetery and read tombstones.

I crossed the street and entered tomb city. Everything was aboveground, either in little houselike tombs or raised brick-bound plots because Limbo is a low island, perfectly flat. Limbs drooped from big live oak trees, almost touching the ground, giving the place a sad look, sort of like Mom's paintings. I hoped they wouldn't influence her art. If she ever got around to painting anything.

Some of the tombs had Spanish names, some Italian or Greek. Color photos in plastic frames were attached to some of the doors or stuck in the ground in little holders. Other photos were faded black and white. I'd seen some of the names on street corners, Hinton, Jones, Bradley, Jenkins, Conklin. Seashells outlined some tombs and the fenced areas.

Other tombs were crumbling. I peeked into one where the door sagged, its hinge broken. Inside I could see the edge of something. A coffin? Spooky.

Suddenly, a figure stepped out of the doorway of a crumbling tomb to my left. Run! my brain said but before I could move, he hurried off in the other direction as if he was afraid of me. Maybe he was homeless and lived in that tomb. Suddenly he disappeared. He was there and then he wasn't. Maybe I blinked, and he fell into a hole. Or a fresh grave.

I checked out the tomb he had been in. The door was slightly ajar, but I couldn't see anything inside that gave it an occupied look. By anybody alive, I mean. The walls were lined with shelves of coffins. Creepy.

This was not a place you'd want to be at night. The sun was still bright, but I jogged back home and locked the door behind me. You never know. I felt goosebumpy, maybe because I'd just read that flyer. And maybe that was why, when Bucky came home from school and said his new friend Billy Brown had some six-week-old puppies and could he have one, I took his side.

"This house is isolated, Mom. I think it would be a good idea for Bucky to get a dog."

Bucky looked at me as if I had just turned into his fairy godmother. Mom looked at me like I'd left my brains in New Hampshire.

"I'd feel better coming home by myself if we had a dog here. It would tell me if it was safe to come in or not. And Bucky would get a lot more exercise walking him." Meaning he might lose a lot of his pudge.

Mom kept looking at me, and I swear I think she was actually on the same planet for a change. After a supper of taco filling on day-old bread, we piled in the car and drove to Billy's house, one of the wooden cottages on Conklin Street. Billy's family seemed normal. He had a younger sister and brother and one each of the usual kind of parents. They all looked alike, so the kids probably didn't have multiple fathers stashed around the country.

"They're part Lab," Billy said of the six tumbling puppies. We picked out a cute squirmy black one. Bucky wanted to name him Blackie.

"Ninety-nine percent of the black dogs in this country are named Blackie," I said. "Try to be a little more original."

"How? How do I be original?" Bucky's trusting brown eyes looked at me seriously.

"Think what else is black. Or we could be sarcastic and name him Whitey."

Bucky thought about that for a while as we rode home, the puppy trying to lick his nose, his ears, his chin, my knees.

"Dirt is black."

"You don't want to call your dog dirty, do you?"

He shook his head and thought some more.

"Soot is black."

"That's the same as naming him dirty. Think of something else black."

"Licorice?"

"That's good. But I think he'd end up being called Licky."

"Okay." Bucky was easy to please.

"That's not such a bad name since he's trying to lick us to death. Think of something else."

"We could call him Lucky," Bucky said.

I had been about to suggest something cute like Inky or cinematic like Darth Vader, but Bucky had thought of Lucky by himself. "Lucky is the perfect name," I said, even though Bucky's dog Lucky sounded like something on TV, something with two blond parents and lots of blond children always getting into scrapes and Lucky and Bucky making everybody laugh at the end.

"Lucky, you're a lucky dog," I said.

Lucky grinned in agreement.

We didn't have any dog food so I soft-boiled the last egg and showed Bucky how to mush it up with what was left of the bread. The pup wolfed it down. Then he licked the bowl and looked up for more.

"Maybe later. You don't want to overdo it. You won't get homemade meals every day," I told him.

"He needs a collar," Bucky said.

And dog food. And shots. We didn't have any spare change right now. Mom was waiting for the right vibes to start her painting career. Meanwhile, she sat in the living room with those Tarot cards spread on the tombstone. She was as addicted to them as Bucky was to his games.

Maybe I could get some baby-sitting jobs. Then I could buy things we needed. Like food. A bedside lamp for my room. I needed new clothes too. It was too hot here for long pants and jeans. I would have to cut mine off. Bucky's too.

I made plans. It was still light out. I had time to walk to the library and back before dark. I made signs to put up on bulletin boards and told Mom where I was going. She placed a card down faceup and frowned. "Not a good sign," she murmured.

I copied down our cell phone number. As I opened the front door, a shadow moved in the cemetery. I caught a glimpse of a man. He looked like the same one I'd seen this afternoon, but I couldn't be sure. Probably a workman. Or somebody cleaning a family crypt.

The man was a workman.

I was sure of it.

He had to be, but in case he wasn't, I was glad we had Lucky.

Chapter 4

I pinned a notice onto the supermarket board and followed the map to the library on a side street. The town was pretty, with gingerbready old wooden buildings, heavy on gift shops. Some of the stuff in the windows looked interesting, and one store had awesome purses. Not that I could buy one, but it was good to know where to go if I could.

As I pinned up the notice on the library bulletin board, I saw Josh pass by. He went into a meeting room around the corner. A sign at the door announced Devil Worship lecture tonight.

What was he doing in there? I almost went in to sit by him. I practiced opening comments. They all sounded lame. Better not risk saying the wrong thing.

The next morning Mom sat on the screened porch, the Tarot cards spread on the picnic table. She'd repaired its broken leg with a stick from the jungle and a coil of wire. Folded cardboard kept the legs from wobbling. She was in her ratty bathrobe again. I hoped she didn't wear it to take Bucky to school. Somebody had to straighten her out.

"We've lived here more than a week," I began, "and haven't been to the beach yet. Can we go today? It's Saturday."

Mom didn't answer. She seemed to be in a trance. Her movements were slow and dreamlike. Maybe she was PMSing.

I tried again. "Could you stop playing cards long enough to take us to the beach?"

"I'm not playing. I'm learning. Tarot is not a game."

At least she answered. I was prepared to beg like a little kid. But first I enlisted Bucky. She seemed to hear him more than she did me. Maybe because he was younger, and her mom instincts were still on for him, whereas I was taller than she was and needed her less. It seemed I'd always needed her less.

I cued Bucky. "Yeah, Mom. Take us to the beach, please!"

She didn't even seem to hear him. This was serious. "More!" I mouthed to Bucky. He really turned it on. "It's Saturday, Mom. Everybody goes to the beach on Saturday."

Bucky was persuasive. The hopeful grin on his round face was hard to resist. He was fresh from his success in getting a dog. He only had to say it three times before she snapped to and heard him.

She scooped up the cards. "Okay."

"Yaaay!" Bucky ran to suit up.

We drove across the island to the public beach. The Gulf of Mexico was clear as tap water but really shallow. I waded with Bucky while Mom picked up shells and stuff. Bucky splashed around while I checked for H and H—hunks and hotties. It was disappointing. I didn't see anything interesting. We had to help carry all Mom's shells and driftwood and parts of old plastic dolls to the car.

"Why'd you get so many shells?" I asked.

"They're free!"

"What about that other stuff?"

"Art projects."

"Um, shouldn't you be thinking about getting a job?" I asked the dreaded question.

"I have a job. I'm an artist."

"Mom, even artists have to eat. And artists' children."

"When have you ever not had food, smart alice?"

I let it go. Maybe I would get some jobs soon. Why hadn't anybody called me? Was there some baby-sitting board you had to pass to get jobs on Limbo Key?

Lucky barked his head off when we drove up. "We should've taken him," Bucky said.

"I don't think he's a beach dog," I said.

Bucky nodded. "Yes he is. All dogs like water."

"There are probably leash and beach laws," I pointed out. "And you don't even have a leash yet."

"I have a collar though." Mom had given him an old red bandanna she used to tie up her hair when she painted. I hoped that wasn't a bad sign—that she'd given away her painting bandanna. It looked better on Lucky, but I didn't say that.

I wished I had a red leash and collar to give him. I went to my room and rummaged until I found the tie to my old bathrobe. "Here, Buckins. You can use this."

He went off happily to walk his dog. I stared at the phone, willing it to ring, but it didn't. Not a single time all weekend. What was going on? I didn't put my address on the notices. Nobody knew I lived on Cemetery Street.

On Saturday afternoon the usually quiet street suddenly filled with the sound of traffic. A long line of cars led by a black hearse drove slowly into the cemetery. Bucky stood beside me watching them. He had never seen a funeral before.

"Coco, what're those cars doing? Is it a parade?"

"Um sorta."

I wasn't his mother. It was Mom's place to explain

those things to him. We found her on the back porch. She was painting the seashells. Pink.

"I found some white and red paint," she explained, a long swipe of paint across her upper lip—like a pink moustache, "so I mixed them together. The shells seemed to want to be pink."

"Mom, what're those people doing across the street?" Bucky asked.

"Well, Bucky, it's where you plant people." Mom actually said this.

"Will they grow more people?"

I went to my room. I didn't want to hear the answer. Something fanciful about people trees, no doubt.

They left for the grocery, and I started on my homework. I was writing an essay for French about going to *la plage* when a siren split the silence and two police cars roared up Cemetery Street. Action! I wondered if somebody was shooting a movie.

I yawned and went back to my essay. What was the French word for wade? *Patauger. Je patauge?* Sounded like something to eat.

Footsteps on the porch. A knock at the door. Our first visitor. A neighbor with hot mango bread? Another Prince Charming for my mother? Lucky she wasn't home.

I opened the door to a policeman. He wore a khaki

uniform with short sleeves and shorts. Neat brown hair, a hint of sideburns, strong chin. "Hello, miss, I'm Officer Parker. I need to ask you a few questions. Do you live here?"

He wore a badge and looked like the real thing, but you never know. Lucky seemed glad to see him, but he might welcome a burglar—though dogs are supposed to be able to smell evil.

"Yes, I do." I let him in but was ready to run out the back door if he was a bad guy. He looked too young for Mom so maybe it was safe, but you never know.

He glanced around the living room and sat on the edge of the sofa. He took off his sunglasses and stared at the coffee table. He looked older without them. About Mom's age.

I sat in a dingy plastic chair that no amount of bleach could whiten. "We found it in the backyard."

He nodded.

I wondered if he was married. He wasn't wearing a ring. He leaned over and scratched Lucky under the chin. Okay, so bad guys can like dogs. Hitler, I believe, loved German shepherds. Officer Parker took out a pad and pen and started asking questions. Who were we, how long had we lived here, had we seen anything suspicious?

"What do you mean, suspicious?"

"People behaving in a way that isn't usual in a cemetery."

"I'm not sure what usual behavior in a cemetery is." I thought about the man I'd seen at the tomb, but he was probably just a workman or a homeless person sleeping there.

He looked at me intently for a long minute, and suddenly I wanted to confess that yes, I'd seen a man twice, though he might not be the same man.

"People putting flowers on graves, cleaning them up, writing down names, making rubbings from the fancier stones," he said.

"I haven't seen anybody over there but workmen. Why? What's happened?"

He didn't answer. "If you see anything, give me a call." He handed me a card from his pocket. It was just like on TV.

"Okay." I saw him to the door and stood looking out after he had driven away. The funeral cars were gone, and I didn't see any more police. What was that all about?

At least Mom wasn't home. Officer Parker didn't know what a close call he'd had at our house on Cemetery Street.

Chapter 5

"Why didn't you come to the staff meeting yesterday?"

Josh was doing something with worms and a jar at our lab station. He slanted a look at me.

"Yesterday was Monday?"

"All day."

"I was—um—busy." I picked up the gift of poo on my seat and stashed it in my purse with the others.

He turned then to look at me. "Were you avoiding me?"

"No. Why should I?"

He really did have the bluest eyes.

"I saw you at the library Friday night," he said. "I thought you came to hear the lecture."

"I'm not into that stuff."

"I'm not either." The right corner of his mouth went up just a little.

Interesting. "Then why were you there?"

"Didn't you read the paper?"

"The school paper?"

For answer, he pulled a plastic sleeve out of his backpack and showed me an article from the *Keynoter*, the island paper.

Dire Warnings from Library Speaker
BY JOSH COLTON

The devil walks among our young people, contends Dr. Gabriel White, who spoke at the Limbo Key Public Library Friday night to a sparse audience. "The devil gets into our young people in unsuspecting ways. By the time parents realize what is happening, it is often too late and their children are lost to them forever."

Dr. White, whose flyer credits him with a degree from Pathfinder College and consulting work with the FBI as well as various law enforcement units around the country, explained how to stop devil worship in its cloven-hoofed tracks. "First, parents and concerned citizens must educate themselves on what this movement is, what it involves, how it affects our susceptible and vulnerable youth. The practice relies heavily on peer pressure once the infiltration has begun." It was unclear to this reporter exactly how the infiltration occurs and who is doing the infiltrating, but Dr. White assures that these topics will be covered in depth in further lectures which will be announced soon. Interested parties and groups may contact Dr. White at his hotel, the Seaside Inn.

I handed the article back to him. "So that's why you were there."

He nodded. "Why were you?"

I explained about the notice on the board and the one in the supermarket. "I guess nobody on this island needs baby-sitters. No one has called me."

"Sure they do. All the time. Did you clear it with the librarian and the store manager?"

"Um, no. I didn't know you were supposed to."

"If you don't, they'll take the notices down. That's probably why you didn't get any calls."

"I thought it was because I live on Cemetery Street." I hoped he would say that didn't matter but he didn't.

"Did you put your address on the notices?"

"No."

"Nobody can tell where you live from your phone number." He refrained from saying duh and changed the subject. "Have you seen anything odd in the cemetery?"

"That's what the policeman asked me."

"Policeman?" His eyebrows went up together like a couple. Very cute.

"One came by Saturday. There was some kind of commotion at a funeral."

He pulled out another article. It wasn't in a plastic sleeve and carried a different byline, Ed Wales. I scanned it quickly. Several tombs had been desecrated with satanic markings. No suspicious behavior had been noticed in the neighborhood. The article was accompanied by two photos showing some kind of markings that looked like stick figures on tomb doors, but they were hard to make out in the grainy pictures. Devil-worshippers lacked artistic talent, it seemed.

"You didn't see anything?"

I was about to mention the man I saw, but Mr. Sherman glared at us and we got busy. It was hard to concentrate on lab specimens when there was a more interesting specimen sitting on the next stool. Twice we bumped elbows because I'm left-handed and he's right-handed. Was he as aware of me as I was of him?

I made a notation in my notebook and put my pencil down. It rolled across the station in front of Josh and dropped onto the floor. Instantly, he picked it up.

"Thanks," I whispered. So he was aware of me. Or at least my pencil. But maybe he was just being polite. Why would such a hottie be interested in me, Miss Poopyshoe, the girl from Cemetery Street? I mean, he could have any girl, probably even seniors. He probably just needed somebody to do scut work on the paper.

Mr. Sherman glared at us again. I got back to work.

Josh was waiting for me after school, his backpack full of books hardly making a dent in his posture while mine turned me into the hunchback of Limbo Key.

"Want to check out the cemetery? See what we can unearth?" He grinned at his joke.

Maybe he was just after a story. I didn't care. It was almost as good as a date. Did people go on dates here? Or did they just hook up? Whatever it was, I would take it. "Sure."

Josh filled me in on his life on the way. His dad was retired from the Army after an injury. His mom was an Army major, deployed somewhere that families couldn't accompany them to, somewhere with a lot more sand than Limbo Key had. "She'll retire in June."

"Will you stay here?" I crossed my fingers.

"Hope so. My dad has a boat that he charters some-times, mostly to service people."

"Service people?"

"Army, Navy, Coast Guard, Marines, Air Force. He fishes a lot. He says he can't get enough of the water. Mom said he should've joined the Navy."

So he wasn't one of the rich kids. Well, not the seriously rich kids. Down here you really couldn't tell them apart from the rest of us. Everybody wore shorts and sneakers or sandals to school. Maybe some wore designer labels, but I don't even bother to read those since I know I can't afford them unless I find them in thrift shops or yard sales.

"What kind of tree is that?" I pointed to a tree like the ones that lined Cemetery Street.

"Gumbo limbo," he said. "The real name of the island is Gumbo Limbo Key."

"I'm relieved to hear that. I thought it meant limbo, like lost in the middle of nowhere."

He laughed. "It's sort of that, too, in limbo in the keys. It's not Key West or Marathon or Islamorada. More of a backwater key, but that wouldn't be such a good name for it."

"I know. It's bad enough living on Cemetery Street." I told him about the locker joke.

"That was Stacy Jaworski. She's okay."

I wasn't so sure.

"So will you write something for the paper?"

"If I can think of something."

"All the assignments for the week were given out Monday, but if you get an idea, you could do it anyway. We can find a place for it."

"Maybe I could do something on locker decor."

"Locker decor?" He worked an eyebrow up. The other one tried to follow. He had lashes like palm fronds. Why did such long black lashes have to be wasted on a boy?

I explained about Stacy's locker, the mirror made to look like a window.

"That would work. It's different. Interesting."

I looked at him. He was serious. "That was a joke."

"So? It's a good idea. Do it."

When he aimed those blue eyes at me, I would probably have agreed to write *War and Peace* for the paper, but I played it cool. "I'll think about it."

We turned onto Cemetery Street, and conversation stopped. It wasn't spooky or anything like that, just a feeling that maybe you didn't want anything to notice you. Nobody was home at our house. That was a blessing. Bucky would have wanted to come with us. Mom would have told Josh's fortune. This way I had him all to myself. We left our backpacks on the porch and crossed the street. The cemetery was empty, no ladies putting flowers on graves or watering anything. No groundskeepers mowing. No gravediggers around. No legs waving out of open graves.

We searched the entire cemetery. It took a long time, but we didn't find any evidence of devil worship or anything else. The cemetery was quiet and seemed peaceful, sort of eternal if you know what I mean. A breeze tugged at the limbs of the live oak trees. Some of the tomb doors had been scrubbed or freshly painted, but a lot of the marble walls and markers had blackened with age or mildew.

"Looks like the graffiti has been cleaned up," Josh said. He seemed disappointed.

"Did you expect fresh markings? A sacrifice maybe?"

"Fun-ny. Do you make a joke about everything?"

"If I can. Does that bother you?"

"No. Beats being sour and glaring all the time."

"Like Mr. Sherman."

"Exactly."

"Do you really think devil-worshippers live on Limbo Key?"

"No. But somebody made those markings for some reason. That's what's important, to find out the reason."

"It could have been a joke."

"Maybe."

"But you don't think so?"

"I don't know what to think. As a reporter, I have to keep an open mind and report the facts, not what I think or feel."

"I prefer to speculate."

"That's called theorizing ahead of the facts," he said.

"Who said that?"

He shrugged. "Sherlock maybe. I read it somewhere."

"So there *could* be devil-worshippers on Limbo Key."

"There could," he agreed.

Chapter 6

Today I would start my new life at Limbo Key High as a journalist, with Stacy as my first interviewee. She seemed distracted when we met at our lockers before class.

"Hi," I said as we opened our doors. She didn't seem to hear me. I opened my mouth to ask her about the interview. Before I could get a syllable out, another girl in the hall yelled, "Stacy, you'll never guess what happened!" Stacy hurried off. I don't know if she didn't hear me or was ignoring me.

Josh didn't mention the article in lab. "No doggy poo today?"

"Nope. Maybe the joke shop was sold out and now has them on special order."

Maybe he'd forgotten about the article, but just before the bell rang he said, "Our articles have to be in by sixth period."

"Um, I don't know if I can make that deadline."

"What's so hard about it?" His left eyebrow wiggled adorably.

I couldn't tell him the truth, that the girl wouldn't speak to me.

"Okay, chief. I'll get on it." I saluted. He returned it snappily.

I rushed to my locker after lab. Stacy wasn't there. I finally caught up to her after the next class. I took a deep breath. "Hey, Stacy," I blurted. "I'm doing a piece for the paper. Can I interview you about your locker?"

"My locker?" She looked at me from under her bangs like I was a fish that had just spoken to her, and whatever was a fish doing in the hall? At least this time she saw me. She seemed to be making up her mind about replying. Then she said, "Okay" but hesitantly, like I was somehow dangerous to be seen with.

I hadn't made up any questions beforehand. I hadn't thought she would actually talk to me, so I had to make some up. Pronto. I pulled out my notebook and turned to a fresh sheet to give me a second to think of something and to make me look more professional. I made a note to buy myself one of those flip pads like reporters use on TV. If I ever made any money baby-sitting, and after I bought clothes, sandals, a new bra, a collar and leash for Lucky, and other basics like food.

I took a deep breath and pretended to consult my

notes. "What gave you the idea to decorate your locker door like this?"

She looked relieved. It was a question she could answer easily. "My mom is really into interior design? I thought it would be fun to decorate my locker door? You know, a room away from home? I'm going to line the rest of the locker with the same paper, as soon as I can get another roll?"

I could never be intimidated by someone who ended every sentence with a question mark. I settled down, and my brain started functioning normally. I took notes and asked her more questions. She seemed easy with them, answering chattily, as if we were friends. Well, not exactly friends, locker buddies. Well, more like locker neighbors.

I wrote a draft during history and showed it to Josh between classes. "I was thinking that maybe we could spotlight a locker every week." I'd noticed some interesting decor as I passed opened lockers.

"That's a good idea. I'll run it by Ms. Finch." He took the draft and raced off without even glancing at it.

By the next day, my status had changed from the lowest of the low to worm level. Only two guys did the Doggypoo Stomp that day. Three people from my classes spoke to me in the hall and they used my name, not some derivative of graveyard denizens. They had probably seen me with Josh. Did this mean that I was on the way to Ms. Acceptable? Maybe I was aiming too high. Ms. Barely Tolerated was more likely.

I didn't have to put it to the lunchroom test. Being broke—Bucky's check hadn't come yet—meant that I had to take a peanut butter and jelly sandwich in a wrinkled recycled paper bag and drink water from the—shudder—fountain. I ate by myself outside under a kapok tree, sitting between the roots that stuck up like shoulder blades, using them for armrests while I leaned against the trunk. On the side facing away from the school, I wasn't visible to anybody, which is how I liked it. If nobody knew where I lunched, maybe I would seem mysterious. The girl from Cemetery Street could dematerialize at will. Heh heh heh.

After school, Josh dragged me to the newspaper room where I met some of the others on the staff—Emily Shute, the editor, Marcus, a tall thin junior who was the senior assistant editor, and Ms. Elena Finch, the faculty sponsor. They were going to use my locker piece with a picture and wanted me to do a surprise interview with anybody I chose each week.

Josh grabbed the paper's camera, and we rushed to Stacy's locker to get some pictures of her standing beside it before she left for home. She seemed really thrilled but that might have been because of Josh. We took the camera back to the newspaper room. Ms. Finch liked the first shot, so Josh put it on the computer.

"It's October now, and we can use some pieces for Halloween," she reminded us.

Spooky stuff was right up my alley, er street.

Josh walked with me as far as Cemetery Street. "See you tomorrow," he said and loped off.

I walked down the middle of the street as usual. Nothing moved on either side of the road, but I had the feeling that things in there could. If they wanted to. You couldn't even see Mr. Gower's house unless you looked way up over the trees and caught a glimpse of the roofline and chimneys. He probably couldn't see the cemetery through that tangle of jungle.

I opened the front door and sniffed. A chemical smell filled the house. Paint. Or something similar. I followed it and found Mom on the back porch. She must have spent the day painting the rest of the shells. About a million pink shells surrounded her on the table. Now she was spraying them with clear stuff and sprinkling them with pink glitter from a salt shaker. "Courtney, you're just in time to help me. As soon as I spray, you sprinkle."

"Mom, what are you doing?"

"Making Christmas ornaments. I got those plastic boxes to put them in."

A carton stood on the floor beside her. It was filled with clear plastic boxes like the ones that cookies come in at bakeries. All the shells had tiny holes so she must have bored them in the shells that didn't already have one naturally. It must have taken forever. I didn't ask what she used as a tool. Mom was pretty creative with odd things around the house: keys, tweezers, paper clips.

While I sprinkled, I told her about my new career at school, but she only said "um hum" and kept spraying.

"This is fascinating and fun, Mom, but what are you planning to do with them when you finish?"

"Margie Muskus at the Jingle Shells Shop said she would take them if they were boxed."

"How much?"

"We haven't discussed price yet." She kept her eyes on the unsprayed shells.

I suspected she wouldn't make much on them. They involved a lot of labor, but they were free and she had plenty of time. Her only costs were the plastic boxes, paint, and glitter. She had enough of the latter to glitz up all of Limbo Key. At least it kept her in a good mood. And everyone should have a hobby, though I knew she considered this part of her art career.

"A Mrs. Ashley called. I think she wants you to baby-sit. Her number is by the phone."

This was really good news. It meant we wouldn't have to eat pet food if Bucky's check didn't come soon. I finished sprinkling the sprayed shells and called the number. I gave Ms. Finch as a reference. She had said I could, and just like that I had a job for Saturday night.

All over Limbo Key notices had sprouted in shop windows and grown on trees for Dr. Gabriel White to speak at all the service clubs, hobby clubs, churches, and even the police department. He was a busy man.

I was busy, too, thinking about the locker spotlights and working on a spooky piece for the Halloween issue. More baby-sitting jobs. Melting my ice floe drip by drip.

I typed my article on the computer in the newspaper room and gave it to Ms. Finch.

Home Is Halloween

BY COURTNEY CARMICHAEL

Halloween is year-round at my house on Cemetery Street. I live across from the Limbo Key Cemetery where the usual traffic consists of the slow, somber corteges following the hearse. Other times the street is enlivened by grave visitors and the backhoe on its way to dig fresh graves. Some of the tombs are very old, dating back to the 18th century with names that recall the early settlers of the island, Conklin, Rodriguez, Hinton, Padilla, Jones. The trees in the cemetery are at least as old as the oldest grave or maybe older, huge live oaks with limbs that seem to reach out, maybe to grab you.

Something squeals in the sky over the cemetery at night. Bats! It's spooky all year round, but definitely not a place you would want to be on Halloween night. Local legends say that ghosts come out of the graves to haunt any who venture through the gates on that night. This is my first Halloween on this street. I'll let you know if any ghosts come to call.

I didn't know if there were any local legends like that, but there were plenty in New England and I was pretty sure Limbo Key had its share. If it didn't, it would.

Ms. Finch liked the piece but suggested that I say visitors to the graves instead of grave visitors. "I'm sure they're grave when they visit, but you want it to read that they were visiting graves," she explained.

So everything was going along swimmingly: Mom busy with her shell-painting, which kept her inside and away from single guys; Bucky with his dog; and me with the paper and baby-sitting and Josh. He wasn't my boyfriend or anything like that, but we did hang out a lot. I was thrilled when Ms. Finch suggested a picture of the cemetery to go with the article and Josh volunteered to take one with his digital. "We can go after school."

"Maybe I should spotlight your locker!"

"Mine's not interesting."

I walked with him to get the camera, and he was right. His locker wasn't interesting to anybody but me. No pictures of girls, I noted. Or boys. Or anything. Just gym stuff, books, notebooks, camera, extra paper, and pens. I bet he even had a little paper clip holder.

"Very neat," I observed in a neutral tone, trying to quell my fantasy of him taking a picture of me for his locker. "Utilitarian."

"I try to be prepared," he said.

"Not totally. No Scotch tape dispenser, I see . . ."

He made a face and laughed. "Who ever heard of a Scotch tape dispenser!"

"I got one for Christmas when I was in elementary school. My great-aunt sent it to me. It was brass." I didn't tell him what I did with it—wrapped it back up in the same paper to give to the teacher that year. We had no money for a gift.

Bucky got home before me. Mom was letting him walk now that she was busy with her shell career. I couldn't see us living on painted pink shells but maybe they would bring in more money than Mom's sad barn paintings had. Or the clothespin dolls. I had treated us to a whole baked chicken with my first baby-sitting money, then bought a red collar and leash for Lucky. It would be easy to get real accustomed to such luxuries.

As we neared the house, Bucky ran out to meet me. He looked worried, his eyes as big as chestnuts under his scrunched brows. "Coco, do you know where Lucky is?"

"No. I just got here."

"He's gone. Why would he run away?" Bucky's eyes filled.

"Are you sure that's what happened?"

"He's not anywhere in the house."

"Maybe Mom took him." The car was gone.

"No, his leash is there. She wouldn't take him without the leash."

I didn't think she would take Lucky with her at all.

"Show us where you left him," Josh said.

"Josh, this is my brother, Bucky. Bucky, Josh."

Josh reached out and took Bucky's hand and shook it. Bucky seemed thrilled. The worried lines over his nose disappeared for an instant. I wondered if anybody had ever shaken his hand before. I didn't want Josh to see our makeshift furniture, but Bucky was off through the house and we followed him to the backdoor. Josh only gave the tombstone coffee table the briefest glance.

"My mom's an artist, sort of," I mumbled, hoping that would explain our hodgepodge of furniture.

The back porch was empty. Mom's plastic boxes and seashells were gone. She'd had me helping her tie each box with pink raffia last night. She must have taken them to the

Jingle Shells Shop. Lucky's bowls lay on the floor empty except for a little water in one. His leash hung from the doll arm Mom had nailed to a piece of driftwood along with two other arms and legs. I saw Josh looking at it.

"Found art," I explained. It sounded better than found furniture, but I was sure he could guess where we got it all. He was polite enough not to say anything.

The door screen was broken down one side and along the bottom. "That's how Lucky got out," Josh said. "Looks like he must have jumped against it."

"The screen was probably old and gave way," I said.

"Maybe." Josh took a close-up of the screen.

"Have you called Lucky?" I asked Bucky.

"All over the backyard," Bucky said. The worried frown deepened.

"You stay here in case he comes back," Josh said. "We'll look in front."

Outside, he said, "Let's check the cemetery. He might have fallen into an open grave and can't get out."

We entered under the arch and called Lucky's name. Josh whistled, but no black puppy bounded up to us. We split up: Josh went to the right, I headed left.

"Here, Lucky, come on boy," I called, and whistled. I could hear Josh doing the same, his voice growing fainter.

And then I found him.

Chapter 7

"Josh!"

He raced over. I could only point. The puppy lay behind a tomb, a dark heap surrounded by a puddle of red liquid. His fur looked wet with what I realized was blood. "He's dead."

"Poor little puppy," Josh said. Then he began snapping pictures.

"What are you doing?" I was angry. How could he think of pictures at a time like this? "That's ghoulish."

"Evidence," he said.

"Evidence of what?"

"We don't know what happened to him," Josh said.

"It's obvious he's been hit by a car. He probably crawled back here to lick his wounds like dogs do and bled to death."

"That looks like what happened, but he's still warm. No cars have left the cemetery since we turned onto the street. The blood is still fresh, and the flies haven't found him yet."

"Flies!" I felt my stomach clutch. "We can't let Bucky see him like this."

"Can you get something to wrap him in? A garbage bag?"

Josh stayed with Lucky while I ran back to the house and found a dark plastic bag. It was used but would have to do.

"Did you find Lucky?" Bucky followed me into the hall.

"We're still looking." I left him on the front porch sitting in the wire chair that had lost its plastic sheathing.

Josh put the puppy in the bag and carried him back to the house. I carried the camera and tried to think how to tell Bucky. Poor little guy. All his life he'd wanted a dog, and now after hardly a week his puppy was dead.

When Bucky saw what Josh held, he understood and his face dissolved into tears. "It's my fault." Bucky shuddered. "I should've taken better care of him."

"It's not your fault. You were great with him." I hugged him as tears pricked my eyes. I wished I could do something to make this easier for him. We should've put a board or something across the screen door, but I didn't mention this to Bucky. It was my fault for not thinking of that. After a few minutes, his sobs changed to sodden gulps. I got a wet towel to wipe his face.

"Are you sure he's dead? Maybe he's just sleeping," Bucky said, hope appearing in his dark eyes, red-rimmed now from crying.

"No, Bucky. He's not just sleeping." I said it gently but my words must have felt like boulders falling on him. He burst into fresh sobs.

"He was hit by a car," Josh said.

"If we'd found him sooner—" Bucky said, gulping.

"It was instantaneous," Josh told him. I wasn't sure about that, but what did it matter now? The puppy was dead.

Bucky sobbed again as if his heart would break. I put my arms around him and sat on the edge of the porch, rocking him, trying not to cry too.

"Do you want to bury him?" Josh asked.

Bucky looked up at Josh. "You m-mean p-plant him like those people in the cemetery?"

Josh nodded. "I always buried my pets."

"Your dogs died t-too?" Bucky sniffed.

"Yes. They were my best friends, and I cried just like you when they died."

"And you buried them?"

"Yes, I did. We can bury Lucky. Do you have a shovel?"

"N-no." Bucky gulped. "We can't even bury him." He cried harder.

"Maybe Mr. Gower has one," I said.

Josh left us looking for a place to bury Lucky and ran to Mr. Gower's house. Bucky chose a spot outside his window where he could see Lucky's resting place anytime he wanted to. I didn't think that was such a good idea, but he insisted. Josh came back with a shovel and soon had a hole at the base of the palm trunk. He gently laid the bag that held the puppy into the hole. Bucky and I picked some orange flowers and dropped them on the bag as Josh began to cover it with dirt. I got some of Mom's unpainted shells to outline the grave like the ones I'd seen in the cemetery. I gave Bucky a jam jar to fill with water and we put flowers in it to set at the head.

"Lucky would like that," Bucky gulped. "It's all neat and everything."

Mom came home then. I told her about the puppy and introduced Josh to her. She twinkled at him and got her Tarot cards out to tell his fortune on the back porch. Josh tried to decline. She didn't seem to notice Bucky's tears but sent me to make lemonade with a can of frozen stuff she'd brought home with money from the sale of shells.

Sometimes Mom just isn't with the program. Maybe if she'd seen Bucky earlier she would have been more concerned. She was telling Josh about fame and fortune and a girl when Mr. Gower came over to look at the screen.

I dumped the frozen lemonade into a bowl. We didn't even have a pitcher. I added water, stirred until it was dissolved, and then had to spoon it into glasses so I wouldn't lose any. Even with ice cubes, we only had enough for everybody to have one glass, and I had to water mine down. I took the mismatched glasses out to the porch in time to hear Mr. Gower say that the screen had been cut.

"Cut?" I stared at him, trying to picture the scenario.

"Who would do such a thing?" Mom said.

"And why?" Josh asked quietly.

"Somebody trying to get in to rob us," Mom said.

I couldn't imagine anybody wanting to rob our house. It was obvious we didn't have anything worth taking. Josh and Mr. Gower were kind enough not to say it.

"Bucky probably interrupted them when he came home," Josh said. "Bucky, you saved your house from being robbed."

Bucky perked up then. After he drank the lemonade he offered to show Josh his collection of shells. Josh was being more of a comfort to Bucky than Mom was. Sometimes I wonder where her brains are.

Mr. Gower called the police to report an attempted break-in, but since nothing was stolen, the police probably wouldn't get around to investigating it for a while, if ever.

Then Mom told Mr. Gower's fortune. When Josh and Bucky came back from looking at the shells, Josh was promising to take Bucky snorkeling.

"I don't know how."

"I'll teach you. It's really easy. All you have to do is breathe through your mouth."

He didn't offer to teach me. I should be happy that he was offering to take Bucky. It would help get him over the loss of Lucky.

Later when Josh had left and Bucky was in bed, I asked Mom why she was so unconcerned about the puppy.

"Everything leaves," she said. I waited for her to explain but she went to her room and closed the door.

Ms. Finch wanted me to work ahead on the locker interviews. I mumbled that I would, but I didn't know what to do. I couldn't just march up to people I didn't know and say I wanted to interview them. I would play it safe. I told Josh he was next.

"My locker isn't interesting," he protested.

"Yes, it is."

"Not. It's not. I know what interesting is, and this isn't it." His blue eyes bored into mine. I stared back.

"That's just it. Every locker can't be like *House Beautiful*." I was making this up on the spot. "Especially most guy lockers. Yours is neat and utilitarian." Like mine, I wanted to say, but I didn't. And sparse, I might've added. It needs at least one picture to give it a focus. A girl. One that you'd like to see often. Like me, for example, but I didn't say it.

He kept looking at me. I hoped he couldn't see the real reason I wanted to interview him was that I didn't feel confident to ask anybody else.

Finally he shrugged and said, "Okay."

We went to his locker after lab. He took the camera off the top shelf and when the hall emptied, I took his picture standing to one side just as he had taken Stacy's for the first article. As I looked through the viewfinder I noticed he had put some pictures up. I clicked the shutter and then moved to get a closer look. He stepped in front of me and slammed the locker door, but not before I saw that one of the pictures was of me sitting in the kapok roots. Did he put it up because of the composition? Or because it was me?

I wasn't as invisible as I'd thought, and I wasn't sorry.

Chapter 8

I plucked courage out of the air and talked to the girl who had the locker on the other side of mine. It wasn't as hard as speaking to Stacy. Aimee was in my French class. The day after I did Josh's locker, I noticed hers plastered with posters of Paris scenes.

"Um, Aimee." She turned. Her eyes were glassy with unshed tears.

"What's the matter?"

"It's that party." She sniffed and plucked a tissue from a pack in her purse.

I never cried over parties. Not since first grade when I realized that I was the only girl not invited to Sissy Bruck's circus party. Mom had been wonderful then. She'd given me the money that I would've spent on a present and let me shop for anything I wanted—candy, a charm bracelet, a plastic horse with a saddle you could take off. I was happy but not fooled.

"What party?"

"Jessica's Halloween party."

"Oh that party." I nodded as if I knew about it.

"I didn't get an invitation."

"There's still time. Maybe it got lost in the mail or something," I said chirpily, sounding like Mom.

"No, Stacy and Carli were talking about it and I heard some of the boys."

"I didn't get one either," I said.

She gave me a pitying look but refrained from saying of course *you* didn't get one because you're *nobody* in this school.

"I'm sure you'll get one," I mumbled in a reassuring tone. I even patted her shoulder. She sniffed as she gathered her books and went off to class.

Funnily enough, Josh brought up the same subject in biology. He was more direct. "Are you going to Jessica's Halloween party?" he asked as we pored over our chart, the day's offering of doggy poo safely stashed.

"Got to baby-sit," I mumbled. It was a lie, but he would be at the party and wouldn't know if I stayed home feeling sorry for myself.

Now that my lunch spot had been discovered, I couldn't go back there. If Josh didn't join me I would feel really bad. I decided to spend some of my baby-sitting money and tackle the cafeteria. Limbo Key High School's cafeteria was no different from any other I'd been to. The noise level was the same and probably the groups too. Popular and unpopular. My stomach felt like it had taken an elevator to Filene's Basement and stuck there as I got in line with my tray and tried to look like I'd been doing this every day. Maybe this wasn't such a good idea. The line moved too fast. I needed a little more time to look things over. Too late. My tray was filled. It was time to find a place.

To sit.

At a table.

One with the least hostile vibes.

Where was my ice floe when I needed it?

I headed for the back where I spied a table with only one person. I dumped my tray at the end. The person looked up. A girl. You can't always tell from the back. I didn't know her, but she was in my English class. One of the pops. I pasted a low-wattage smile on and said, "Hi."

She mumbled something around her cheeseburger just as a group swarmed the table. "Carli, you were supposed to be saving this table."

It was Jessica—the most popular girl in the class. She looked down at me. I gave her a medium-wattage smile. "Hi!" I chirped, amped way down from my conversation with Aimee.

One of the other girls said something to her. "Oh hi," she said. They all sat down. Fortunately there were enough chairs or they might have made me give up mine.

I speared lettuce with my fork. So far this had been relatively painless. Then they started talking about the Halloween party. I chewed my lettuce and the single slimy wedge of tomato that made my lunch into a salad and tried to think serene thoughts. It was hard because I've always hated it when kids talked about a party that a person within earshot could hear about but wasn't invited to. It's just rude rude rude. I wasn't a nobody at this school. Well, not a total nobody. I wrote for the *Gumbo*. It was time for me to take a stand.

"Jessica," I began.

The table froze. Jessica's fork stopped halfway to her mouth.

"Are you inviting the whole class?"

Jessica looked at me as if I had suggested inviting death-row denizens. Our eyes locked. She was the first to look away. The fork entered her mouth. She chewed.

"Your point is?" It was Carli. She waited for my reply, her fork held in the air like a pitchfork aimed at me, a chunk of avocado hanging precariously from the tines.

I ignored her and watched Jessica chew. A girl I didn't know sitting on the other side of Jessica whispered something to her. All I heard was something about the paper. They didn't know if I was asking for myself or for the paper—an item, maybe in Bloggo. "Sophomore girl has big Halloween party, guest list restricted." She chewed the question and her cheeseburger for a nanosecond longer, then swallowed.

"Well, sure," she said uncertainly. "Everybody in the class."

Carli sucked in her forkful of avocado, but she looked like it didn't taste all that good.

Why hadn't I done this before? Was it something in the tropical climate that gave me the nerve? It was so easy. I tried to analyze what had made the difference. This was the first time I had ever been involved with anything extracurricular at school. This was the first time I hadn't slunk around the halls on my ice floe all the time. Maybe Jessica didn't want anything in the paper about a party that everybody wasn't invited to. Or maybe she was just a nice girl and hadn't realized how it sounded to those not invited to hear about her party. It was something for me to think about.

"That's awesome," I said and gave her a lot of watts.

Later when I was being bored to death in algebra, I remembered that other girl whispering in Jessica's ear. Had she told her I'd been seen with Josh? Had the word got out? I hoped so.

When the paper came out on Friday with the interview of Stacy, more people started speaking to me. I got up the nerve then to ask Aimee to let me interview her. She seemed pleased.

As I opened my locker at the end of the school day, Stacy actually spoke to me of her own accord. "I really liked what you wrote about me in the article. My mom will like it. Thanks."

I studied her eyes. She seemed to mean it. I smiled back. Trickle, trickle.

As I was leaving, I ran into Josh.

"How's Bucky?" He asked that every day.

"Still crying himself to sleep. Mom tried to find him another puppy. Billy gave all his away."

"Did she try the animal shelter?"

"They didn't have any puppies. Mom even called as far away as Marathon Key."

"I'll ask around. Meanwhile, would he like to go snorkeling tomorrow?"

"He'd love it!" I would too. Josh wasn't dense. How could I make him see this without coming out and telling him? "Why are you being so nice to Bucky?"

He looked at me. "Why wouldn't I be? He just lost his dog. That's a hard thing on a kid. I remember how it felt. And maybe because I know what it's like to move around a lot, with your dad gone. And your mom too, sometimes."

Why was he being so nice to *me* was what I really wanted to know. Did he like me because we had rootless-ness in common? And single parenthood? I hoped those weren't the only reasons. I mean, as girls go, I'm really okay. I have shiny hair that tends to chestnut, and green eyes. I could use more curves, but Mom says people gain weight when they're older and I should be glad I started off slim.

"Bring him over in the morning." Josh wrote an address on a sheet he tore out of a notebook.

Did that mean I was invited too? I decided I was.

Did this count as a date?

Bucky was so excited I didn't think he would ever get to sleep that night. At least he wasn't crying. Mom was out, and I had to stay home with him. Luckily I didn't have a sitting job. When I asked where she was going, she didn't answer. She was dressed up in a swingy skirt and big hoop earrings, lots of bracelets and necklaces. Did she think this would attract her soul mate?

"Don't you think you should be looking for a job?" There. I finally said it.

"I have a job."

"I mean one that brings in revenue."

She just looked at me and went on stroking eye shadow on her lids. Bronze that brought out the frosted green in her eyes. She left before supper, saying she would eat at the Bait Shack. What? Stir-fried bait? Creamed worms? Fricasseed cricket? For once, smart alice kept quiet. It was the first time she had been out at night since we moved here. I didn't want to discourage her, but I needed to caution her.

"Don't get married," I called after her.

"Don't be—"

"I know. A smart alice. Do you want me to be a dorky dora? Or a loopy lucy?" I got more creative. "Or a milquetoast molly?"

She stood in the hall and stopped pawing through her purse for her keys. She looked up and gave me a blinding smile. "Don't be any of those. Just be yourself."

"It was a joke."

"Oh. Ha ha then." And she was gone.

Actually I was serious. Mom's been single now for more than a year. That's a record. It also meant that she was ripe for another wedding. I had to be on the alert.

Josh's house was on an inlet across from another islet. Bucky and I walked across Limbo Key in our bathing suits, but I wore lemon shorts and a lime T-shirt over mine—thrift shop finds. Bucky wore a plain white T-shirt over his. I knocked on the door of the weathered gray house. It looked like it had been built out of driftwood.

Josh let us in and introduced us to his dad, an older version of Josh. The house was airy with wonderful views of the Gulf of Mexico, water color and oil paintings on the walls, a lot of white wicker furniture with squishy pillows in shades of blue and green, lots of ferny plants in baskets, a wall of books.

"Bucky's not much of a swimmer," I said. "I don't think he can even dog paddle."

"Anybody can dog paddle, but you don't have to swim to snorkel," Josh replied. "Anyway, we're not going in water that's over his head."

"I thought you had to dive down to reefs or something."

"No, that's scuba-diving. We're just going to lie on the surface of the water. The fish are mostly in the turtle grass where the water is shallow. All you have to do is look down like you're in a glass-bottomed boat."

I didn't tell him we'd never been in a glass-bottomed boat.

Josh gave Bucky a mask, tube, and fins. "Those were mine when I was younger."

Hero worship was instantly born. "I been wanting to snorkel my whole life," Bucky said.

Josh grinned. "You can use my mom's." He handed me a set and picked up one for himself.

On the beach I slipped out of my shorts and flip-flops and started to take off my shirt. Bucky skinned his off. "Leave them on," Josh told us. He was wearing a white one over his dark red suit. "When you're lying on your stomach your back will be exposed, and it will blister really fast."

That was fine with me. My old white suit was frayed around the edges. My wardrobe was as threadbare as our lives.

He showed us how to put the snorkel through the mask strap and how to spit on the inside.

"Spit!"

"Keeps it from fogging up."

After choking a few times, trying to breathe through our mouths, Bucky and I got the hang of it. We spent the morning floating around looking at angelfish and striped ones that Josh said were sergeant majors and purple and gold ones that called beau gregories grazing in the turtle grass just a foot or two below us. We never went deeper than three feet. It was amazing what you could see and how clear it was.

"I'm ravenous," I said when we stopped around noon.

"What's that mean?" Bucky asked.

"Starving," Josh said.

"Me too then, what Coco said."

Mr. Colton had left pimento cheese for sandwiches

and deviled eggs in the fridge. We sat on the back deck to eat. Our bathing suits and shirts dried quickly. Then Josh said he would walk home with us.

I slipped into my shorts and we took a different route home. A few blocks away, Josh led us around to the back of a house stuccoed in soft rose with white shutters. It was tucked into neat beds of tropical plants blooming their heads off, orange, red, coral, pink. He knocked on the backdoor.

"Mrs. Salvadore," he called.

Yippy little barks came from the backyard. I looked speculatively at Josh, and he smiled.

A tall woman in white shorts and a green T-shirt came to the door. "Hi, Josh. Is this your friend?"

He introduced us, and she took us through a little gate into the backyard where three puppies leaped about with more energy than a rock group.

"Two of them are promised, but this little fellow needs a good home." She picked up a squirming puppy and held him out to Bucky.

He stood there in mute disbelief for a moment, his hands at his sides.

"I-I can't t-take him," he said in a low voice, looking at his feet. His bottom lip wobbled. He was about to cry.

"Why not? He seems to like you already." She held the puppy close to Bucky. The pup licked his arm.

"I didn't take care of my other puppy, and he got runned over," he said in a low voice, almost a whisper.

"I'm sure you'll take good care of this one. Here, he wants you to hold him."

She thrust the puppy into Bucky's middle. He was forced to put his arms around it or be licked to death.

"Mr. Gower replaced the screen, Bucky," I reminded him, "and he said he has a board we can put across the door."

"See, you can just take him right home with you now," Mrs. Salvadore said, smiling at Bucky encouragingly. "The pups are part Welsh terrier among other things. He'll be a very smart dog."

"Thank you," he whispered, his arms closing around the puppy.

Josh walked home with us. I carried Bucky's snorkel gear. He carried the puppy. We stopped at Mr. Gower's and showed him the dog. He gave Josh a wide board to carry home for us. At the house Bucky put Lucky's collar on the pup.

"What're you going to call him?" Josh asked as Bucky snapped the leash to the collar and led the pup around the yard.

"Power Ranger," Bucky answered quickly.

Josh and I looked at each other. Bucky had picked a strong name. I wanted to hug Josh for making my little brother happy again. As he was leaving, he looked over at the cemetery. "Seen anything over there?"

"Not really."

"What do you mean not really?"

"Sometimes I think I see lights, and sometimes I think I hear stuff."

"What kind of stuff?"

"I don't know. Chanting maybe, but it's probably just the breeze in the banana trees or parrots or something."

"Probably."

Neither of us sounded convinced. I tried to picture chanting parrots.

Chapter 9

Our life on Limbo Key seemed to settle down after that. I found some pots curbside and planted them with pothos I found growing wild behind the house. I put one in an old basket on the tombstone in the living room and another in my room. Kept the air clean, I read somewhere.

Things were going great for me at school, with Josh and the paper. Mom seemed better too. I couldn't see that she was doing anything creative now that she had finished all her shells, but at least she was more active. She went to the Bait Shack almost every night. What could she be doing there? Was she selling worms? Crickets? Baitfish? Did people buy bait at night? I guessed they did if they went night fishing. I finally asked if she had a job now.

"Sort of."

At least she was out of that ratty old bathrobe. That was progress.

Bucky had Ranger. And I had—what did I have? An article every week. A sort of friend who happened to be the wowiest boy I'd ever talked to. Mom seemed to have more money now—maybe more of her boxes of shells had sold—so I used some of my baby-sitting money to buy shorts and shirts at the local thrift store for Bucky and me. I even found a pair of Jagcats like new that fit if I laced them tight enough.

As I walked down the halls at school, I began to notice things besides who had interesting locker decor. I liked that there weren't gangs or cliques in the school aside from the popular and the not. The school was small enough so everybody knew everybody else. I also liked that few kids had cars. Almost everybody walked or rode a bus or bicycled. A few had mopeds.

I noticed couples too, the ones sneaking into the custodian's closet or under the auditorium curtains, behind the stacks in the library, though Mrs. Gilbert had a sharp eye for anything more than a quick kiss. I saw Stacy watching a senior football player, Gary Harper, when he passed our lockers. Yearning. Poor Stacy. He would never look at her. He was dating a girl in his class, Rita Smith. I could almost see Stacy's heart thumping as she looked at him. I hoped I didn't look like that around Josh. Carli was going with a junior named Sammy. Moira liked Alan, but so far he didn't seem to know that.

Aimee stayed aloof, but I saw her watching Devin in French. So far I hadn't seen Josh going with anybody. Or Jessica.

I asked Aimee about him in French.

"He doesn't go with anybody now," she said, pasting a moustache on for the skit we were doing. She played a garçon in a café. I was a French poodle. I'd borrowed Ranger's dog collar but it was so small that I had to use a rubber band to hold it on. I had a curly pink wig on my head and had tied pink bows on my wrists and ankles. I had also painted my nails hot pink the way some people paint their poodles' nails.

"What about before now?"

"Jessica was his main squeeze all last year. Is my moustache on straight?"

"Straight enough. What happened?"

"It slipped."

"No, I mean with Jessica and Josh."

"They broke up in the summer. I don't know why. I think she dated somebody else while he was away crewing. There's your cue."

"Les chiens, avez-vous faim?" Devin said.

"Woofee! Woofee!" I said in a French accent as I pranced into the café, but I was thinking. Does Jessica go with somebody now? Or is she still interested in Josh?

More important—is he still interested in her?

And the bigger question—is he interested in me or are we just colleagues? Fellow reporters?

The plastic doggypoo continued to appear on my lab stool. I tried to get there early every day to whisk it out of sight before anybody saw me. Today I wasn't fast enough. Josh saw. "Guess the joke shop got in a new shipment," I said.

"Is it there every day?"

I nodded.

His eyebrows went up, but the bell rang and we got to work. Mr. Sherman was a tyrant.

On Friday as I picked up the offering, Josh said, "You must have the biggest collection of plastic poo on Limbo Key."

I smiled, but it was a grim smile. One could get tired of some things. "I'll bequeath it to the Limbo Key Museum."

He laughed. "You going to the game tonight?"

Had he been about to ask me to go with him? "I have to baby-sit for the Lanas."

"Do you baby-sit every Friday night?" He worked on that eyebrow. It quirked just a little.

"So far." I hadn't been to a single game, not even the ones played at home. I didn't want to sit by myself in the bleachers. Anyway, I needed money. So I baby-sat on weekends and during the week if anybody called and wasn't going to be out too late.

"What about Bucky?"

"If Mom's out, I take him with me. He doesn't like it because he has to leave Ranger. He loves that dog so much," I rattled on. "He asks about you all the time. He says, did you tell Josh that Ranger went all night without peeing on the floor even once? He was so proud of that. I'm surprised he didn't ask me to put it in the paper."

Josh laughed. "Maybe he'd like to snorkel again."

"He'd love to," I said. Me too. But I didn't say that.

"Bring him over tomorrow about ten."

It wasn't exactly a date, and nobody would see us, but I would take it.

Then he asked about the cemetery. I could only report that I hadn't seen anything. I didn't look over there if I could help it. I couldn't erase from my mind the picture of Lucky, the bright red blood, the pitiful scrap of puppy.

I certainly wasn't invisible at school. I had Josh and the newspaper job to thank for that. I'd got to know the paper staff and the yearbook staff across the hall. For my fourth article I picked the locker of a freshman, Bitsy, who had a crush on Dominic Monaghan. She was a little girl barely up to my shoulder. That's probably why she liked him, a hobbit in *Lord of the Rings*.

The inside of her door was papered with pictures of him and the inside walls as well. You couldn't see even a sliver of the gray metal. When I asked her why so many pictures, wouldn't one do, she said no.

"When I open that door, I'm surrounded by him. It makes me feel, feel—" Her eyes traveled to more pictures on the ceiling. She seemed to be searching for the right word up there.

"Transported? Happy? In love?" I offered. "Safe? Comforted? Comfortable?" I amended.

"Comfortable. That's it—it makes me feel comfortable." She smiled, and that made her brown eyes stand out. I could imagine that a girl smaller than most of the freshmen would feel lost in high school. The locker decor was her security blanket, but I wouldn't put that in the article. I arranged to take her picture after school when nobody would be around to see. The locker interviews were secret, and the interviewees had to promise not to tell until the paper came out.

"Courtney, your Halloween piece will run in the paper this week," Ms. Finch told me after I had taken Bitsy's picture and turned the article in at the *Gumbo* room. "We'll run the picture of a tomb that Josh took."

"Already?" Where had the month gone? Suddenly I realized that Jessica's Halloween party was a week from Friday. And I still hadn't been invited. Maybe she considered me a rival for Josh. I kind of liked that idea.

On Friday, Dr. Gabriel White came to speak to the

morning assembly. Josh was covering it for the *Gumbo*. I sat next to him and tried to pay attention, but Jessica sat in front of me. Before the speaker was introduced by the principal, Ms. Johnson, Jessica turned, looked at me, and gave me a half-smile. What did that mean? Was she gloating about her party? Or was it meant for Josh?

I didn't listen to Ms. Johnson's intro. I'd read the credentials on Dr. White's flyer. He got up and thanked her in a deep voice with a surplus of flowery words. Then he gazed at us sternly. "The devil is all around you!" he thundered.

Somebody snickered. It was hard not to. He fixed us with a deep scowl, raised his right hand, and pointed a finger at the audience. "You may laugh, but the devil is invisible. And he takes the form of people you know. You could be sitting next to him right now."

This time the snickers were suppressed, but we had trouble hiding our grins. We'd seen all those movies about stealing shapes and souls. We weren't falling for that line.

"How does he know the devil is a he?" I whispered to Josh. He wrote it down.

Dr. White's eyebrows shot way up and he opened his eyes really wide to emphasize a point. He looked almost demonic himself, his black hair electric. I wondered if he dyed it.

"These were beliefs held in the past, but Satanism is not just a quaint event that happened in Salem in 1692. Satanism is alive and well in this century. Look around you at your neighbors. They may be practicing it secretly while going to church on Sunday. Why should you be concerned, you say? Because Satanism is a serious crime, a gateway to drug use, vandalism, theft, sadism, even murder."

I was glad I didn't have to write an article about this assembly. I tuned Dr. White out and stared at the back of Jessica's head. Her hair was long and curly, but like most of us she had pulled it into a ponytail to keep cool. It was longer than mine and swished when she moved her head. I thought about the party I wasn't invited to. I didn't know about Aimee. She hadn't mentioned it again, so maybe she'd been invited by now. I didn't want to bring it up in case she hadn't or in case she had and then asked me if I had. Maybe Jessica would invite me if I interviewed her about her locker. My thoughts ran around like squirrels. I could hold Bitsy's interview for another week and put Jessica in for the Halloween issue. But that was sort of blackmail. I wouldn't do it.

I wondered what the inside of Jessica's locker looked like.

Dr. White's speech broke into my thoughts. "This is not just some isolated event. These cults are rampant in our communities! In your community! Right here on Gumbo Limbo Key. They vandalize graveyards. They stalk our most defenseless, our children. They stalk you. And you. And you." He pointed to the right, to the left, to the middle.

I've never seen any vandalism, but there were those satanic markings that the police had investigated. Okay, so maybe there was one Satanist on the island.

At the end of his talk, the students had a lot of questions for Dr. White. Beside me, Josh was scribbling furiously in his notebook. He raised his hand. "Is Halloween a time when people are particularly vulnerable to Satanic crime?"

I was impressed. Most of the questions had been lame, like how can you recognize a Satanist, do they smell different, that sort of thing. I snickered to myself as I thought of Eau de Brimstone. Evening in Sulphur. Did they wear Satan Red nail polish?

"Halloween is the most vulnerable time of the year but all of the solstice dates are important events and times of increased Satanic cult activity."

One of the teachers asked how we can protect ourselves.

"Read my books. I am donating a copy of one to the school library. Others will be on sale at the end of the hour and in stores in town."

Ah ha! That's why he's here. To sell his books. I didn't realize I had said ah ha out loud, but Josh glanced at me and even Jessica half turned and caught my eye. What did that mean? Did she think I was right? Or a dork?

The bell rang for the end of the hour. "You buying one of his books?" I asked Josh.

"No way." He grinned.

"I thought you were really into that stuff," I teased.

"It's my assignment. I have dibs on the library copy for the article. Then I have to interview Dr. White. Why weren't you taking notes?"

"Me? Why would I take notes?"

"Ms. Finch wanted you to cover a different angle from my article, which is straight reporting."

"Nobody told me."

"I thought I told you." He frowned at his notes. "Guess there was a mix-up, but you can do it. Or I can ask Jessica."

I didn't want to confess that I'd hardly heard a word of the man's speech, but no way was I going to give up and let Jessica do it. "Oh sure. Piece of gateau. I'll think of something," I mumbled as we went to our classes.

But I couldn't. I couldn't think of a thing. Not while I was baby-sitting at the Lanas' that night. And not as Bucky and I walked to Josh's house the next morning.

Bucky was pretty cheerful now, with Ranger to keep him busy with walks before and after school and several in the afternoon.

I didn't tell Josh I couldn't think of a thing to say about Dr. Gabriel White except that I thought he was a nutcase who maybe wanted to scare people into buying his books.

Bucky had wanted to take Ranger with us to Josh's. I managed to persuade him that Ranger wouldn't have anything to do while we snorkeled.

"He could swim."

"Not for as long as we snorkel," I said.

So we left Ranger chewing his rawhide bone on the back porch. I made sure the board was across the screen door. Maybe somebody had cut it before, but I didn't want to take a chance that Ranger could rip the screen and run away.

After about an hour floating above coral castles and turtle grass forests, Josh and I sat on the deck and drank iced tea. Bucky didn't want to quit so we watched him while a warm breeze dried our wet shirts.

"I showed those pictures I took of Lucky to a vet I know," Josh said. "She said she couldn't be sure just from looking at pictures, but there were no injuries consistent with a dog that small being hit by a car."

"What about a moped or bike?"

"Same thing. She said it looked to her as if the dog's throat had been deliberately cut."

The Gulf of Mexico still sparkled. Bucky was a little boy islet floating on it, but suddenly he looked fragile and I worried about a boat swerving into the curve of Josh's inlet. "Who would do such a thing?"

"That's what the vet said. I've been checking into animal crimes. The answers vary. Disturbed children. Teen vandals. Satanists."

I shivered in the breeze that didn't seem so gentle now. Even on this island paradise, evil could lurk. "All three are horrible," I said finally.

"All are aberrant behaviors." He looked at Bucky. "Sometimes pets are taken as a lure."

Chapter 10

Mom was in her ratty bathrobe again, slapping cards down on the picnic table, when we got back from snorkeling.

"When are you going to start your art career?" I asked as I rinsed our swimsuits out and hung them on the back porch line. "When the vibes are right?"

"Don't be a smart alice." She didn't even look up.

I didn't reply to that. I didn't think she had any real artistic talent but I would like to see her keep on working at something. I mean people usually get better when they work at something. The first rocks she painted were a blobby mess but after she had done a lot, they started looking like blobby scenes. Maybe somebody would buy her shells. Maybe she would become a painted shell artist. And maybe Josh would take me to the Christmas dance and I would be crowned Miss Sophomore Queen. I swallowed my snicker.

Maybe she heard more than I thought. "I finished all the shells. Margie can't take any until more sell."

"Painting shells isn't art. That was the reason we moved down here, right? You wanted to be an artist."

She looked up then. "There are many paths to art. We have to find the right one."

Sort of like finding a soul mate? I didn't say it. "That sounds a bit vague. I'm sure other women artists didn't sit around waiting for the path to show itself. Georgia O'Keefe. Or Mary Cassatt. Or—" I tried to think of more examples.

"Georgia O'Keefe married a famous man. Mary Cassatt came from a rich family." She slapped a tarot card down on the picnic table.

That shut me up. Poor women probably didn't become artists a long time ago but this was now and there was nothing stopping my mother. She had paint. She had time. All she needed was something to paint on. She could probably find some interesting driftwood. I would look for some next time we went snorkeling. Maybe it would get her started.

When I came out of the bathroom after my shower, she was gone. So were the cards. Maybe they were leading her to her path. "Where does Mom go at night?" I asked Bucky.

He shrugged, intent on brushing Ranger. "Out?"

I took Bucky with me to the Moores'. They had two wild little boys under four and Bucky was great with them. They played pirate ship until the little boys fell asleep on the boat, first one, then the other, and I put them to bed. We dismantled the ship made from ottomans, chairs, and other bits of household things. I picked up the stuffed rabbits and bears that doubled as sharks. Then Bucky fell asleep on the sofa and I was left alone to watch TV. The Moores had cable. I forgot all about the article.

By Sunday I still hadn't thought of anything to write about Dr. White. Worse, I couldn't think what to do about Jessica and the party. If only I knew whether she'd forgotten to ask me or if she was trying to blackmail me into doing an article about her locker.

Monday morning she was opening her locker as I passed on the way to mine. The door swung back and a jeweled bat sprang from a coil inside. The school didn't allow painting the interiors of our lockers but she'd lined hers with shiny black paper and made webs with silver Silly String or something that looked like it. Here and there jeweled spiders clung to the web. Another jeweled bat hung in the corner. A ghostly howl followed by laughter came out of the depths. I had to admit that this was one cool locker. Should I do it?

"Hey, Jessica."

She turned and raised her eyebrows at me. I didn't

want to ask her then because people were all around us. I went to my locker and wrote her a note. When I got the chance later after lunch I slipped it to her. She read it and nodded.

Okay, I was giving in, you could say. It wasn't like I was selling my soul to the devil or anything like that. Her locker was way cool. It would be terrific for the Halloween issue. And it was my duty to the paper to put the articles above my own feelings. And the possible blackmail. Journalism ethics, Josh would say.

At the paper staff meeting Ms. Finch asked me about my article on Dr. White.

"I'm working on it." I scrunched up my face to look like I knew something about what I was doing. Ms. Finch seemed to buy it. She moved on to the next assignment.

When the hall emptied after school, I took Jessica's picture with the paper's camera. I asked questions about her inspiration for the locker decor. She was a little stiff at first.

"How did you make those silvery webs?"

"Liquid solder and Silly String. I wanted it to be spooky and glam at the same time." She half-shrugged. "Scarecrows and ghosts are not my thing."

"Why spiders? These are really glam but who would've thought of it?"

She grinned and sort of opened up. "We're into spiders at my house. My little sister Emma is scared of them. To help her get over it, Mom got her a stuffed one with sequins all over it. Now she waits for the live spiders around the house to grow their diamond scales as she calls them. She wants to be a spider for Halloween. She's four and says funny things like that."

I wrote it all down including the stuff about Emma. It was good copy.

"Do you plan to keep these decorations all year?"

She shrugged again and fingered the jeweled bat. "I don't know. I haven't decided. I might take the bats down after Halloween but keep the spiders. For a while anyway. Who knows, maybe I'll think of something else to do for Thanksgiving. I will definitely change it for December."

"I wish the picture could be in color," I said. "At least it will be on the on-line version."

"I wish I could wear my costume in it. I'm going to be a slinky spider." She struck a slinky pose and I snapped her.

"Somebody might see us. Remember it's supposed to be a surprise. Anyway nobody else has been in costume for the articles." It was enough that I was putting her and her locker in the paper. No way would I put slinky spiders in this issue! The interview was as far as I was prepared to go.

I waited for her to mention the party. I'd asked her

all the questions I could think of. There was nothing left to say. I glanced at her to see if she was gloating, but she seemed unconcerned as she collected books from her locker. She slammed the door shut as I started down the hall and fell into step with me.

I tried to think of a way to bring up the party without actually saying anything about it. Where was my brain when I needed it? Finally I said, "Can you believe all the homework tonight?"

"No, I hardly have any and I did it all during class."

"Why do you have those books?" I nodded at the three she was carrying.

"Oh these are from the library. They're about spiders—for Emma."

Okay, so she was nice to her little sister. That didn't help me.

I returned the camera to the *Gumbo* room as she went off to her popular life.

I ran into Josh outside the school. "Did you do the article on Dr. White yet?"

"It's not finished." I couldn't confess that it wasn't even started, that I didn't pay attention to the talk and had no idea what to write about. I had a feeling that Josh would consider that a sin.

"E-mail it to me if you finish it tonight. My address is Josh@lol.net."

"Lol?"

"Limbo on line."

"Cute." I didn't even know LOL meant laugh out loud until Bucky told me. I thought it was some kind of condition like ADD or acne. How embarrassing is that to have your little brother know something you don't know?

"Um, problem. I don't have a computer, but I'll have it for you in the morning."

"Okay. My article is almost writing itself. That guy is one piece of work," Josh said, following.

Was he walking home with me again? Could this really be happening? And where was Jessica? "What do you mean?"

He stopped and looked at me. "Do you think there are devil-worshippers on the island?"

I stopped too. "I haven't lived here long enough to form an opinion. What do you think?"

"No, I don't. I've only lived here two years myself, but I've never seen any evidence."

I didn't mention Lucky. There'd been nothing to connect his death with Satanism. As if on the same wavelength we both started walking again. "What about those markings in the cemetery?"

"It could've been ordinary vandals trying to scare people."

"You're probably right. What are you going to be for Halloween? Scary or cool?"

"Haven't decided yet. You?"

"Also undecided." He didn't ask again if I was going to the party.

We got into a discussion of why people chose the costumes they did. A car went by. A silver car. I didn't pay attention until the back window went down, and Carli Fuselier stuck her head out. "Hey, lover boy, you gonna carry her books home to the cemetery?"

Another head just beyond hers chimed in. "That would be a grave mistake," followed by peals of laughter.

"What'll Jessica think? Gone but not forgotten."

More braying.

I thought I caught a flash of Jessica in the front seat but couldn't be sure. I cut my eyes to Josh to see how he was taking it. He stared straight ahead, but I detected a slight redness under his perpetual tan.

"I think people show off their true selves all the time," he said as if we hadn't been interrupted. "But when they put on costumes, they flaunt part of themselves they may not know is in them."

I disagreed. "I think people know what's in them. They just don't admit it to themselves because then they would have to face something that isn't likeable to them." Like my mom and her multiple marriages, her aimlessness. What was the root of all that? The loss of my father? Orphaned at 12? Having a baby at 16? Not finishing school? Mom wasn't stupid. I mean, she reads a lot. Or she used to. I hadn't seen her reading in a long time.

We talked about it until it was time for me to peel off to Cemetery Street, but essentially Josh and I agreed. One thing we decided was that boys like to wear costumes that are scary or powerful. Girls like to be pretty or scary. I thought that scary girls' costumes were the same as power costumes because witches have power. And slinky spiders.

By the time I reached our house, I knew what to write my column on. Costumes. What did devil-worshippers wear? Did they have a Best-Dressed Devil-Worshipper's list? Did they all wear basic black? Red? Unisex? I would start with Salem, then go into Halloween costumes and use our discussion. I was halfway through writing the article when Mom brought Bucky home. I didn't even hear them. I was so into it. I kept the tone light. I didn't believe Dr. White's theory, and I wasn't going to let him get away with his scare tactics.

It took more than that to scare me.

Chapter 11

I can't believe I did it. Last night I called Josh and read the article to him over the phone. I've never called a boy before. I know, I know. Girls do it all the time. I just never had the nerve.

I agonized for hours but when I finally did call him, it turned out to be no big. He liked my idea for polling a random sample of kids about costumes, and the next morning we did it together and then wrote down the specific costume but not the name in case it was a secret.

Ms. Finch said my article made a good companion piece for Josh's. He didn't give Dr. White a free ride in his article either, but reported fairly what the doctor had said, including my question about Satan's gender. She liked the costume poll and after we compiled the data, Josh and I worked on it together.

"Did you ever decide on a costume for Halloween?" I asked him when we had handed in the survey article.

"Not yet. Are you dressing up at school?"

"Maybe. If I can think of something." I didn't have the money for one costume, much less for two or three like most kids had.

After school I looked for Josh. When he didn't appear, I trudged off by myself. A car just like the one Carli had been riding in the day before passed. The windows didn't go down. Nobody shouted anything at me. I wasn't worth noticing. Maybe Carli had scared Josh away. With a sinking feeling I realized I was back on that ice floe, and I would have to work to keep afloat.

When Bucky got home, I took him to the Spritely Used shop in town. Right away he found a red Power Ranger suit that was only a little too short for him. The mask had been cracked and mended with glue, but he didn't care. I couldn't find anything. Next we went to Goodwill, where I found a short red hooded cape. I could be Little Red Riding Hood at school. I bought a basket for 25 cents. I wished I had a red dress to wear. Did Little Red Riding Hood wear a red dress? I couldn't remember. I settled for a red-and-white checked tablecloth that I could make into a skirt with some elastic. It was only 50 cents because it had a hole in one corner, but it wouldn't show when I turned it for a waistband. For another dime, I got a matching napkin, the only one in the store. I could make it look like I was wearing an apron. I stopped in Publix and bought a roll of slice-and-bake chocolate chip cookies to fill my basket with goodies in case anybody looked.

I made the cookies after Bucky went to sleep so he wouldn't want a fistful. I stitched up the tablecloth by hand and ran some elastic from an old pair of pants through the waistband. The next morning I put it on with a white blouse and tacked the napkin to the front, tucking it into the waistband. I tied the cape around my neck and put my hair in two ponytails. I had already packed the cookies and lunch in the basket and spread some of the leftover tablecloth over it.

A rabbit, Pocahontas, two butterflies, a clown, several Power Rangers, and a bunch of Harry Potter, Lord of the Rings, and other fantasy characters, a trio of girls dressed like cats, and a Cinderella converged at the entrance when I got to school. A jumble of kids in costume milled around in the hall, characters from books and movies, and at least two teachers were dressed as Ms. Frizzle. The vice principal was Ichabod Crane or something from Dickens. It was hard to tell. Ms. Johnson was Glenda the Good Witch from Oz. Moira was Paris Hilton with a blond wig and a limp pink dress with spaghetti straps. At least I think that's what she was, though she could've been Barbie.

Jessica said she was Queen Elizabeth I, but she could have been Miss America if she'd had a sash. Suzanne wore a green ballet costume with a fake emerald and diamond tiara. Bitsy wore a fairy princess costume with gossamer wings and a sparkly crown. Carli was Ariel with a tight fishtail skirt she could hardly walk in, seashells in her hair, and a swimsuit top she had sewn with two huge shells and lots of sequins, jingly shell bracelets and necklaces. I had to admit it was a pretty good costume. Aimee wore a slinky black skirt, tights, high heels, sweater, and beret. She looked très French, especially here on this tropical island, and she was already sweating. One thing I didn't see was anybody in a bear suit. It'd definitely be too hot. Even real bears didn't even live this far south. Right away people started humming or singing bars of a song about Little Red Riding Hood when they saw me, and I did a little dance step, not the doggypoo stomp.

"Going my way?" A wolf came up beside me after French class. His rubbery lips were stretched in a wolfish leer. He danced a few steps with his giant wolf feet and waved his wolf paws. I pretended to dance away in fright.

"Josh! You came as a wolf! What made you pick that?"

"It's an old costume. There was a red cape, but Dad gave it to Good—." He stopped abruptly.

I laughed. "Then it was fated. I went there looking for a costume yesterday afternoon and found it. This was all that was left." I hadn't tried any of the retail stores, but Josh didn't know that.

"Our fate awaits." He crooked his arm for me to take, and we pranced down the hall together as kids with cameras and cells snapped us.

Ms. Johnson was videoing the hall. When she turned the lens on us, Josh said in a British accent, "I say m'dear, what do you have in your basket there? Goodies, by any chance?"

"Why yes, Mr. Lobo. How did you guess? I was taking them to my grandmother, but if you'd like to share them with me for lunch, Granny can wait until tomorrow."

"Raw-ther."

And we pranced into lab.

"Do you want to? Have lunch with me?" I couldn't believe I actually said this!

"Sure. I'll get milks and meet you at the kapok tree."

I looked at him, but he was still wearing that silly mask and I couldn't read anything in his wolf face.

Josh had pushed his mask up on his head by lunchtime and discarded his paws but he still wore the giant wolf feet. We leaned back in the cubicles formed by the kapok's roots. He propped those giant feet on one of the roots. I put the basket between us and Josh lifted the handkerchief. "Yum, my favorite pimento cheese—and homemade. How did you guess?"

"It was fated."

We laughed. I'd brought deviled eggs too and plenty of cookies. The day seemed happy and silly and full of laughter, the best day I'd ever had at school. Maybe anywhere. Hands down the best Halloween.

That afternoon the paper staff distributed copies of the Halloween issue and then everybody went back to the *Gumbo* room. Josh and I had left enough cookies to go around and Ms. Finch had brought orange punch and chocolate cupcakes.

Josh walked to Cemetery Street with me. Maybe he hadn't been bothered by Carli's taunts after all. He'd removed his wolf stuff and slung it over his shoulder in a bag. I had folded my cape up in the basket.

"Are you wearing the same costume tonight? I'm not going to be a wolf again. Not in costume anyway." He leered adorably.

"No." I might as well tell him the truth. "I'm not going. I, um, have a job." It was sort of the truth. I was baby-sitting myself. I hadn't taken a job because I'd been hoping I'd be invited to the party.

"On Halloween?" He raised both of his eyebrows.

"It seemed important," I explained. Maybe the invitation would be in the mail when I got home. Maybe a miracle would happen.

It didn't. Jessica couldn't say she didn't know where I

lived. No, she had left me out deliberately, the only one in the class not invited.

"WHAT DO YOU MEAN I HAVE TO BABY-SIT BUCKY?"

"Stop yelling," Mom said as she poured a glass of water from the fridge pitcher.

"I'm not yelling, I'm being emphatic. Why do I have to baby-sit him?"

"Because I got this great gig at the Capstan Key Hotel."

"Gig?"

"Engagement."

"What does that mean?" Did she have a date? Was she about to get married again? "You could've told me before now." I didn't know what I could've done about it, but with more time maybe something would have popped into my brain.

"It was a last-minute thing. The entertainment dropped out of the Halloween Ball—had an emergency appendicitis or something. Mr. Gower recommended me, and I've been engaged to tell fortunes. It's more money than I've been getting at the Bait Shack and the beauty parlors altogether. It could be the start of a new career for me."

"Appendectomy. Emergency appendectomy." I stared

at her. "*That's* what you've been doing all this time? Telling fortunes?"

Mom nodded. She had a pleased-with-herself look. I thought she'd been hanging out at bars and here she'd been earning money telling fortunes. My mom does a lot of weird things, but this was the biggest surprise she'd ever handed me. Fortune-telling!

"I told Mr. Gower's fortune that day, you know," she inclined her head toward Ranger, "and he suggested I do it at the Bait Shack."

"You've been telling the fortunes of people buying bait? What do you tell them, you will have great luck at the end of the sandbar sort of thing?"

"Don't be a—"

"I know. It's a joke. But seriously, Mom, do people get their fortunes told when they're buying bait? Aren't they in a hurry to get their lines in the water or roar away in boats?"

"Where did you get the idea the Bait Shack sells bait? It's a very good restaurant, famous in the Keys."

"A restaurant? The Bait Shack? Why would somebody call a restaurant the Bait Shack? It makes me think of worms and crickets and crawfish. Certainly not something to eat." I made a face.

"Maybe it once sold bait. Or maybe it was to entice customers. I'll ask George next time I go there."

George?

She went in her room and closed the door. I sat at the table staring at the yellowed walls of the kitchen. George. Was she about to get married again? I made jokes about it a lot, but they were just jokes. Most of the time.

Bucky came in from walking Ranger. The puppy had grown about a foot and was hungry all the time. I opened a can of dog food for Bucky to put in his bowl.

Mom twirled across the hall. "I bought a new outfit. How do I look?"

She glittered in a swirly skirt, black with gold moons, suns, and stars sprinkled all over it and tiny round mirrors that caught the kitchen light and brightened up the dim room. The full-sleeved blouse was sheer black, and she wore a lacy black camisole under it. She'd tied a sheer black scarf around her hair and put on lots of gold jewelry. She carried a small twinkly purse. My mother the bling queen. No fortune-teller in the world ever looked that glitzy.

"Great. You'll knock 'em dead."

"You look pretty, Mom," Bucky said.

And she did. She hadn't looked this happy in a long time. Since the last time she got married. "Don't get—"

"I know, married," she said, laughing. "It's not in the cards right now." She hugged Bucky and dropped a kiss on my head. "Wish me luck."

"Everybody will want their fortunes told by the glamorous fortune-teller."

"Yeah, Mom," Bucky said. "What she said."

She was gone, leaving me to baby-sit Bucky.

I groused to myself while I warmed a can of pasta for Bucky. I poured it into a bowl and plunked it onto the table. Time for him to start learning to cook for himself. I knew how to warm things when I was his age. Even younger. "Come and get it," I said loudly. Maybe I yelled it. He rushed in and slid into his chair. I poured a glass of milk and put it on the table. Tossed on the rest of a loaf of bread.

"Aren't you gonna eat?" he asked when I stood leaning against the sink, my arms folded in a classic aggrieved pose.

"I'm not hungry. I had a big lunch. Maybe later."

He had draped a towel around himself to keep food off his Power Ranger costume. Maybe he was learning to think ahead. I watched him chew. Noisily. He was eight now. Too old for that. I'd have to teach him a few things. But tonight was Halloween. No reason to spoil it for him too. "You want to go trick or treating?"

"I'm going to a party at Billy Brown's."

"You're going to a party?" I raised my eyebrows and gave him a look. "Mom didn't say anything about that."

"Guess she forgot." He reached into the bowl on the

table where bills and things were tossed. A pumpkin-shaped invitation announced the party at 6 P.M.

I looked at the clock. It was already 5:45. If I hurried, I could get him to his party in time. I rushed him through brushing his teeth, and we left for the Browns'.

Their house was decorated with lighted ghosts, pumpkins in windows, a witch on a broomstick running into a tree. Mr. and Mrs. Scarecrow sat on a real bale of hay. Where did anybody get a bale of hay on Limbo Key?

"The party is in back," Bucky said.

The backyard was decorated more than the front of the house and filled with more Power Rangers, Ninja Turtles, and action figures with a few skeletons and at least one vampire. Mr. and Mrs. Scarecrow were alive back here. I recognized Mr. and Mrs. Brown under their patchwork costumes. The girls were all in princess costumes except for one Pocahontas, several witches, and a little bee who must be somebody's little sister, and one mummy who could have been anybody.

I left Bucky bobbing for apples. I would come back for him when the party was over at 9:30.

Chapter 12

I walked slowly back to the house on Cemetery Street. It seemed emptier and more forlorn than ever, even with Ranger there. The jungle around the house was dark. The cemetery was dark too.

I probably should've eaten something, but I wasn't hungry. Everyone else in the class was getting dressed for Jessica's party. I felt really sorry for myself. Like Cinderella. Where was my fairy godmother when I needed her? Where had she ever been? Ranger thumped his tail and grinned at me. He could be my coachman. Or maybe the lead horse. We didn't even have a pumpkin. I should've bought one for Bucky.

This was Halloween night, and I was home by myself. I'd stood up for the nerds in the class, and I still wasn't invited to the party. Now they were all having fun at Jessica's. Everybody was having fun on Limbo Key tonight except me.

Suddenly it came to me—my most brilliantly audacious idea ever. I would crash the party! I could dress up. They might not recognize me in costume. I would be a mysterious stranger. Like Cinderella, I would leave the party before it was over.

What could I wear? I knew not to bother looking in my closet. I pawed through Mom's, looking for inspiration. Her wardrobe was pretty pathetic too. I found a light blue dress. With an apron, hair band, and stuffed cat I could be Alice in Wonderland.

No apron. No cat. No time to get either. And that wouldn't be much of a disguise.

I looked for a slinky black dress. Mom must have a slinky black dress somewhere. How else did she get all those husbands? I could be a witch, carry our broom. No black dress, but I did turn up the black crushed velvet skirt she'd been wearing to tell fortunes. It was almost as swirly as the one she was wearing tonight. I could be a fortune-teller just like Mom, but I needed a top. Where was the red one she'd worn with the skirt? I checked the hall closet. Not there. The bathroom? Nope. The line on the back porch. She'd hung it high so Ranger couldn't reach it. I dug some scarves out of her drawers, tied a long orange one around my waist and a purple one behind my ear.

I wore all her leftover gold junk jewelry around my

neck and both wrists and slid on a ring with a huge fake green stone. Big hoop earrings completed the look. Black flats. I went heavy on the glamour makeup. Smoky mauve eye shadow. I looked at myself in the mirror. My eyes seemed bigger and also sexier with Mom's eyeliner and false eyelashes, contouring blush on my cheeks. My mouth too seemed to have changed shape with lipstick instead of the light lip gloss I usually wore. I hardly recognized myself. I dusted my hair with gold glitter.

The cemetery was quiet as a grave as I stepped off the porch. I left the light off so trick or treaters wouldn't come here. The night was dark, not even a glimmer of a moon. I walked as fast as I could.

I found Jessica's house easily. It was the most decorated on Gulf of Mexico Drive. I had looked her up in the phone book. I didn't want to end up at the wrong party.

The house was white, two-story. I could hear the party in full swing somewhere in back of the house. I walked up the drive lined with glowing jack o'lanterns, real ones carved in grimacing faces with real candles lighting them. More lanterns grinned out of the windows. A witch rode a broomstick from the upstairs porch. She swayed in the breeze along with ghosts swooning from the railing. A raccoon about half my height opened the door. It pointed around back. I followed the jack o'lanterns.

I stood on the edge of the party and felt myself

freeze. I didn't recognize anybody. The costumes all seemed fancier than mine. I counted at least seven witches, and they were the glamorous kind—lots of bling, and flowing, slinky black dresses. A sequined spider girl about the size of the raccoon danced in a circle of graveyard ghouls and vampires. She must be Jessica's little sister. Where was Jessica? Where was Josh?

Plastic ghosts floated in the pool. Tiny purple lights glittered in the bushes and trees. Silly String webbed the shrubbery, accented here and there with jeweled spiders. It was the most decorated party I had ever been to. I recognized Jessica's touch.

I searched the crowd until I saw her ladling punch, a glamorous spider glittering with jewels. Her dress was black with caped webbing between the bodice and sleeves. She was talking to a tall boy in a cape. He grinned and showed his fangs. It wasn't Josh.

Was it?

A woman I figured out was Jessica's mom, dressed in a glittery pink Marilyn Monroe costume, noticed me. "Oh, I'm so glad you were able to make it," she cooed. "Come this way."

What did she mean? She didn't know me. I hadn't even been invited, but I followed her to see what would happen. She led me to a tent set up on the side of the yard. A sign over the entrance read Fortunes by Madame

Zizou. Inside stood a table covered with a shiny purple cloth. She lit the candle in a bronze lantern and set it on the table. A silver spiderweb floated over my head.

"Do you need anything else?" she asked as the tent glowed with soft candlelight and dancing shadows. "I wanted to use a skull lantern, but I couldn't find one."

"This looks fine," I assured her.

I guess she thought I was the fortune-teller she'd hired for the party. I started to explain that I was Jessica's classmate, then I worried if Jessica recognized me I might have to leave. That would be so embarrassing. I could just imagine what Carli would say.

Maybe I could be the fortune-teller. I wished I'd paid attention to Mom and her Tarot cards. Wasn't it all just mumbo jumbo? If Mom could do it, I could too. I slid into the chair at the table. Somebody had pinned silver cardboard stars and gold moons and suns to the hem of the tablecloth. I moved the lantern to one side to throw shadows on my face. Maybe nobody would recognize me. I flipped the ends of the scarf so they'd fall over my left cheek and sort of shadow my face more.

A man entered the tent. My first sucker, er victim, I mean customer. What could I do?

He sat in the chair across from me and looked at me expectantly. He wore a baseball suit. "You must be Jessica's dad."

"Hey! You're good," he said with a grin.

I didn't tell him the uniform said DiMaggio so he must be with Marilyn, which made him Jessica's other parent. Elementary deduction.

"Did you bring your crystal ball?" He looked around as if I was hiding it somewhere in plain sight.

"Sorry, the cat knocked it off the table and broke it." I didn't have any Tarot cards and wouldn't know how to use them if I did. "I'll be reading palms tonight. The ball is just a prop anyway. Um—focal point." Get with the program, Courtney.

"Okay, here's your next customer." He left as a tiny spider entered. It had to be Emma. An easy one. "Welcome, little spider, to my tent. Give me your—" What did spiders have? Not hands or paws. Legs? "Give me one of your front legs."

She giggled and put her hand on the table. "Ah, I see a delicious fly stew for you and—oh, here is some chocolate fly pudding."

She left in giggles, pleased with my prediction that she would have a famous career training spiders for the circus.

Then Aimee entered in a French cancan outfit. I waited for her to recognize me. When she didn't, I looked in her palm and spoke in a whispery voice with what I hoped sounded like a foreign accent. "Ahhh! I see a journey across water to a land where they speak another language. Something hovers over you. An erector set. No, not a toy. Big."

"The Eiffel Tower!" she almost shouted.

I felt a pang. I shouldn't be doing this to Aimee who had been nothing but friendly to me. And then I thought that it was all in fun, I was only adding to the spirit of the party. "I see a windmill in a strange color. Orange, no— red."

She nodded. "The Moulin Rouge!"

"You will meet a handsome student at a famous university."

"Is it—is it the Sorbonne?" She looked so hopeful that I hoped my predictions would come true for her. I could see how dangerous fortune-telling might be. And what a responsibility.

"Your palm cannot tell me that," I backtracked. "You must follow your path to find out."

She left, entranced, the future sparkling in her eyes. More followed, all girls. I made up more stuff. I told Stacy she'd go to Hollywood on a family vacation, and the car would get a flat tire in front of Channing Tatum's house.

"Then what?" she asked breathlessly, and I realized that she had entered into the spirit of the fun.

"Ah, your palm cannot tell me that yet. You will have to grow a little to reach the next installment. Come back in four months and I will look again."

This was fun.

By now I had abandoned caution and really got into it. I told Jessica that a blond stranger would enter her life soon, maybe tonight, that her lifeline had many branches and each would make a lot of people happy. What I really wanted to say was basically unprintable. She left, satisfied, and didn't seem to recognize me either.

I told Carli she would marry a man with glasses, "a very serious, grave man," I added with a straight face. "You will have two sets of triplets." She giggled, and didn't even get the grave jab.

The boys came then. Derek from my French class would travel the world before settling down with a French-speaking girl. And John from history would have an accident at a historical site, but would meet a mysterious stranger who would involve him in a lifelong career. I told so many tall tales that I couldn't even remember what I'd said. I probably repeated myself. Nobody seemed to notice. It was all in fun.

A tall boy in desert camouflage came in wearing night vision goggles that gave him the look of a monster. I kept my head down and half-whispered, "Please to remove the insect face."

He pushed them up on his head. They left red goggle lines on his face, but at least he couldn't see me any better than the others.

"You have a very interesting lifeline here. It doesn't go straight but meanders a bit. However, your loveline is very deep. It keeps you on track."

He laughed, and I looked up. He grinned. "What else, Madame Zizou?"

I looked down at his hand, trying to think of something witty to say. My mind was blank.

His wasn't. "Why didn't you tell me you were the fortune-teller?"

Josh had recognized me right away!

"Because I wasn't." I abandoned Madame Zizou's voice and spoke flatly in my own. "I wasn't invited to the party. I crashed it. Jessica's mom thought I was the fortune-teller she'd hired who apparently couldn't make it. I didn't tell her any different."

He frowned. What had I said that was wrong?

"Everybody in the class was invited."

"Uh uh. Not me."

"I'm sure you're wrong. Jessica's not like that."

"She obviously is. Why are you defending her?"

"I'm not defending her. I just want you to be fair."

"Fair?" My voice went up.

"Jessica isn't perfect, but she wouldn't leave anybody out."

"Maybe the Jessica *you* know wouldn't leave somebody out, but the Jessica *I* know did, and I'm living proof."

His eyes were dark in the shadows. Navy blue. "Are you jealous of Jessica?"

"Jealous?"

I looked down at his palm, which I was still holding. I didn't want him to see my tears of anger. He turned his hand over. The face of his watch shone like a moon in the shadowy darkness. I read the numbers upside down. Almost ten.

Bucky! I'd forgotten to pick up Bucky!

Without a word, I jumped up and ran out of the tent. I heard a crash behind me. I didn't know if it was my chair or if I'd knocked the table over. I didn't stop to find out. I ran between all the costumed dancers.

"Hey, where's the fire?" a ghoul said as I passed him.

I ducked around the clustered revelers and raced to the street. I ran all the way to the Browns', my heart pounding along with my feet. "Please be there, Bucky," I said aloud over and over.

The night was black as sin. Most of the houses on the streets had turned off their lights. By the time I reached Billy's, I had stitches in my side.

The house was closed up. The pumpkins had been blown out. The party was over.

Where was my brother?

Chapter 13

I raced home, trying not to panic. I'd let Bucky down. I'd let Mom down. How could I ever fault her again when I was worse? It was too soon to cry. Bucky would be there waiting on the steps for me. He had to be. I clung to that thought as I turned into Cemetery Street.

A long shadow detached itself from the porch. "Bucky! Thank goodness you're home. I'm so sorry. I forgot the time."

"It's me, Josh. Where did you go, Cinderella? I ran after you and thought you'd come home, but when I got here, you weren't here. Why did you run away?"

I was never so glad to see anybody. Only Bucky would have made me gladder. I laughed at his joke, but it turned into a sob. "Have you seen Bucky?"

"No. Nobody was here when I got here."

I unlocked the door, calling, "Bucky! Bucky!"

Josh followed me as I checked the house. I just knew

I would find him in his bed asleep. His room was the last one next to the back porch and across from the kitchen. It was empty, his bed untouched.

"Where's your mom?"

"She had a job at the Capstan Key Hotel."

"Was he home by himself?"

"No, of course not." I explained. "I thought he probably walked home when I wasn't there to pick him up."

"Would he have gone trick or treating?"

"No and anyway, it's too late for that."

"Could he have got lost in the dark?"

I didn't want to think about Bucky lost and alone in the dark. "I don't think so. He knew the way home from the Browns. Where can he be?" Desperation made my voice rise. I was close to tears again.

Ranger whined and scratched on the door to the back porch. I let him in. He ran all over the house looking for Bucky.

"We can use Ranger to track Bucky. Where's his leash?"

Instantly relief flooded me. Of course, Ranger would find Bucky.

Josh snapped the leash on Ranger's collar. We left by the front door.

"Find Bucky, Ranger, find Bucky," I said over and over.

Ranger looked up at me. His brow furrowed like he

was thinking hard. His eyes were bright and alert in the porch light. He put his nose to the ground and sniffed.

"Look, he knows what I'm saying!" I was thrilled and proud of Ranger at the same time. He would find my brother. "He has Bucky's scent! Ranger will find him." At the sidewalk Ranger ran around like he was following a trail of Silly String.

"He's picking up the scents where Bucky walked him today," Josh said.

"He needs to move on. Let's go, Ranger, find Bucky!"

Ranger looked up at me.

"Find Bucky, boy!" I implored him.

He put his nose down, then ran to a tree and lifted his back leg.

"Maybe he's too young to track," Josh said. "Come on. We'll have to look for him."

We crossed the street. I didn't want to take time to put Ranger in the house so he went with us. Maybe he could get a whiff of Bucky.

Josh pulled his goggles down and powered them up as he started across the street.

I balked. "Don't go in there, Josh, Bucky wouldn't have gone into the cemetery. He was afraid of it."

"Maybe he saw something over there. Or maybe he went in with friends or on a dare," Josh said over his shoulder. "It's still Halloween. Trust me, little boys do things on Halloween they wouldn't do at other times."

I didn't think Bucky would have gone in there even with Mom, but I followed.

The cemetery was silent. The only sounds were our feet on the crushed shell road. We didn't have a flashlight or even a candle at home. I was glad Josh had those night vision goggles. I held onto him because if he got a few steps ahead of me, I wouldn't be able to see him.

"Maybe we should call him," I whispered.

"No." Josh didn't explain, but I understood. It was scary in the cemetery. We didn't know who might be listening. Or what. I couldn't stop my brain from thinking that.

Visions of ghouls and monsters crowded my head. I didn't need those images. I concentrated on not tripping. I tried to feel ahead with one foot, but we were hurrying so I stumbled a lot. Josh did too, even with the goggles. We kept each other from falling.

Josh veered off the road to the left, into the darkness between the tombs. I held onto his hand with my right one but my left bumped against the corners and walls of the tombs, and once I stepped into a sunken place. I let out a yelp. Josh grabbed me so I didn't fall, but I banged my knee hard against a wall.

"We're in the oldest part of the cemetery," Josh whispered. "Some of these tombs have crumbled."

"Maybe he—" I began, but Josh cut me off with a sharp *shhhh*.

"We don't know who might hear us," he said in my ear, and I felt a chill that went all the way down my spine. The monster parade played again in my brain, plus some additional devil-worshippers like the ones Dr. White had talked about. Apparently more of my brain had been paying attention that day. What I hadn't heard, I could imagine. That scared me even more. I clutched Josh's hand tighter and kept close to him, brushing his shoulder when he slowed. We had Ranger. He couldn't do much, but at least he could bark and maybe that would scare anybody off. Or anything.

Something thumped in the dark. Something close by.

"Did you hear that?" Josh whispered.

"I heard a *thump*."

"I think it came from a tomb."

"Where? Where is he? Bucky!"

Another *thump* sounded in the dark to our right. Josh and I felt around. We were surrounded by tombs, but in between were graves in raised plots with little walls about shin-high. A lot of these had snaggly headstones, fallen headstones, statues of different sorts. I couldn't think of a worse place to look for somebody at night. Except maybe a swamp with quicksand. And snakes. And alligators.

"Bucky?" I whispered.

Thump. I felt that *thump* under my fingertips touching a cold stone.

"Something's inside," Josh whispered.

Ranger made snuffling noises.

"Where? Inside what?" I hoped he wouldn't say what I thought he was going to say.

He said it. "In this tomb."

His words crashed down on me, and for a second I could hardly breathe. My next thought was, "Is it Bucky?"

"I don't know."

"Maybe he crept in for some reason, and the door shut on him."

"I don't think so. Feel." He placed my hand on something cold and hard and metal. A padlock. A locked padlock.

"If he's in there, he didn't accidentally get locked in."

"Exactly."

"Somebody locked him in."

"Right," Josh said. "And we have to get him out."

"How?"

"First we have to make sure he's still in there. I'm going to take Ranger around the tomb to see if there's a way out the back. Wait here."

"No, I'm coming with you." I grabbed his arm again and slid my hand into his.

Josh led us around the side, both of us feeling for a door or an exit of some kind.

"Nada," Josh said after we had gone all the way around.

"Are you sure he's in there?"

"You heard the *thump.*"

I banged on the door with the flat of my hand, a soft thudding sound. "Bucky, are you in there?" I whispered urgently.

Josh used his fist to beat a muffled tattoo.

Nothing.

"He may not be in there. If he is, and he isn't making any noise, he may be——" I gulped back tears and couldn't say the word.

"No, he's not dead," Josh said. "If he were, Ranger would be howling or something, the way dogs do. He's excited. He knows Bucky's in there and alive."

I wished I could be as sure as Josh. "Bucky, Bucky, Bucky." I beat on the door and kicked it. If he was in there, why didn't he answer?

"Stop." Josh took my hands in his. "If he's in there, he must have heard us. Maybe he can't answer."

I felt myself freeze and slumped against the tomb. Josh was still holding my hands. Ranger snuffled at our feet and bumped the door.

"Did you hear something?"

"What? I didn't hear anything but Ranger."

Josh let go my hands and scooped Ranger up. Something bumped the door again. From inside.

"It's Bucky! It has to be."

"Bucky, can you hear us?" Josh said in a loud whisper. "It's Josh and Coco."

Something thumped again.

"It is Bucky! Buckins—hang in there. We'll get you out. Just—"

A hand clapped over my mouth. In my excitement, I'd forgotten to whisper.

"I don't think we *can* get him out. Not without a tool. Can you find your way back to the house with my goggles and call the police? I'll stay here with Ranger and Bucky."

I nodded. He slipped the goggles over my head. I tried to fight until I realized that I could actually see through the goggles into the blackness of the cemetery. I could see Josh's face but not clearly. Everything was sort of greenish and shadowy.

"Hurry! Bring back a tool."

"What kind of tool?" We didn't have things like that.

"Any kind. Hammer, screwdriver, pliers, bazooka."

I gulped back a nervous laugh. "Okay."

Suddenly my vision was hidden by something soft

like hair and something brushed my lips. Was that his hair? Or a kiss? It was hard to tell even with night goggles.

"Be careful," Josh said. He squeezed my hand. "Better call the police."

I jogged away. With the goggles I could see the tombs and not run into them, I thought, and then I hit my knee on a low headstone that had almost toppled over.

"Ouch." I didn't break stride but rubbed my knee as I kept going.

I thought I'd reached the road that crossed the one to my house but it was only a gap in the tombs. I looked back to see how far I had come and when I turned around, I saw something moving through the tombs. I slowed to a walk, then stopped.

A figure rose between the walls. Where did it come from? An open grave? An occupied one? The shadowy figure got bigger. It was moving closer. TOWARD me! I took a step back and hit a wall. The shadow advanced. I would have to run. I lifted my right foot ready to bolt, but the shadow leaped to close the gap between us.

Too late!

The shadow loomed over me. It was shaped like a man, but didn't look like one. I could see its horrible features now. The face had cadaverous holes for eyes and a gaping mouth. The face of a demon. I opened my mouth to scream, but nothing came out. As the shadow closed on me, the demon's mouth got bigger. It lowered itself to my level. I reached upward to push it away, but my arms wouldn't move. The demon blocked my vision, and then I was falling backward into an abyss of blackness.

Walls rose around me. Steep walls. I scrambled to my feet, amazed that nothing seemed to be broken. I'd landed on dirt. The walls were above my head, and I couldn't reach the top. Where was I? I looked up and I saw the strip of stars above me. I had fallen into a freshly dug grave.

Then the stars disappeared, and darkness slid over me.

Chapter 14

Did I faint? How do you know if you've fainted? Everything was black. I couldn't remember anything except that demon face and the walls of the grave. Was I still in there? I touched my face. The night goggles were gone. I was lying on some kind of floor. I felt the cold and grit through my clothes. I sat up and for a minute my head swam. I couldn't see anything. I tried standing. My legs were a little rubbery, but they held me up. Where was I? I began to explore.

And then I wished I hadn't as my hands touched cobwebs and shapes I didn't want to think about. I knew where I was now. My brain shied away from the word but even without naming it, my fear portals were wide open and shrieking though nothing came out of my mouth. I was in a tomb.

Alone in a tomb.

Alone in a tomb with skeletons and dead people.

And spiders.

And maybe snakes.

Probably no alligators. That's a relief, but I screamed anyway. The pent-up screams that hadn't got out before went out now. The sound was earsplitting in that enclosed space.

Entombed. My mind flashed on all the mummy movies I had seen and then went through all the horror movies as well. Freddy was there. He grinned horribly at me. I couldn't stop the images. Maybe the brain does this to show you that your situation is way less horrible than movies, but my brain wasn't fooling me. I knew that those were movies. This was real.

I was locked in a tomb. Then I remembered Bucky. My poor little brother. I cried for him. I hoped he wasn't as scared as I was. He hadn't seen any horror movies. Maybe he thought it was a game like more serious hide-and-seek.

And Josh. Where was he while I was locked in a tomb? He was waiting at the other tomb with Ranger. He expected me to bring help. When I didn't come back, what would he do? Go to the house for help? Would he make it? Or would the demon get him too?

Then my brain went over the edge into a place blacker than this tomb. I lost it then. The sound that came out of my throat was from the gut, a howl like a trapped animal. "Noooooooooooo!"

My teeth chattered with numbing cold. I wrapped my arms around myself to try to keep warm, but icicles went through me.

"Stop this." I said it out loud. The sound of my voice reassured me for about a second. Don't lose it, I told myself. I only had to stay sane for a little while. Somebody would come by eventually, and I could shout and be rescued and then we would rescue Bucky and Josh. Or not.

If the demon had locked Josh in a tomb, maybe it was the same one Bucky was in. They would at least have each other. Bucky wouldn't be so scared. Especially if Ranger was there. I was alone in this tomb. I hoped.

Why couldn't the demon have locked us all in one tomb? Wouldn't that have been more efficient? Maybe the three of us and one little scrap of a dog could have figured out an escape plan or something. Did demons think logically? I was alone. I didn't have much chance of getting out, but I had to try. I couldn't stand here frozen with fear. My fingers found the door. Not good. Heavy wood. Locked. I kicked it a few times, but the wood was solid. Unmoving. Hinges too. "Help!" I yelped.

My yells fell on dead ears. There was no such thing as demons. I knew that. I'd been locked in this tomb by someone impersonating a demon. The darkness seemed to thicken. If I ever got out of here, I'd never let myself get boxed up again. I will get out of here. I will. Somehow.

Time passed, but there was no way to measure it. Minutes, hours. I sang softly to myself for a while, but with all the yelling and fortune-telling, my throat felt raspy. Jessica's party seemed so long ago.

I felt myself mutating. Like a fish in a cave losing its eyes in the perpetual dark. Would I lose my voice too? Would I become nothing but a pair of ears before it was all over? I could already hear things I'd never heard before, strange hissing sounds, tiny grating ones, and pulsing sounds. Scrabbling. Crabs? Things with claws. New sounds joined the others. A key slid into a padlock, turned.

Josh! He was picking the lock to rescue me! It would be just like a romance novel. I prepared to swoon into his arms. The door opened. I couldn't see anything. "Josh?"

I opened my mouth to take a deep breath of fresh air. A length of tape was slapped over it just as my hands were taped behind me. No blindfold. That was good. I didn't need a blindfold. I couldn't see anything anyway.

A solid black shape propelled me in front of it through the tombs. It was that demon again. I was out of the tomb but still in the graveyard. The dead zone.

My eyes detected a faint glow ahead. Dawn already? And then we turned a corner to a little cleared space among the tombs. The demon shoved me down. I fell over something. Something alive. It moved under me. Josh!

I struggled to sit up. Bucky lay on the other side of Josh, his back against the same tomb Josh leaned against. They were both taped, too. I smelled something smoky, acrid, and turned to see a small fire. That was what made the glow. And then I discovered there were two demons. The taller one seemed to be the head demon, the other a sort of henchman demon. An Igor.

Josh leaned over and touched my cheek with his to reassure me that we were in this together. It was oddly comforting.

The demons converged on us, and I saw their faces clearly now. They were white with large black holes where their eyes, noses, and mouths should have been. Skeletal beings. They taped our feet and then picked me up, one at my head, one at my feet. What kind of demon uses tape? Human demons, that's who.

I kicked as hard as I could but with both feet together, it was more like bucking. It was no use. I couldn't get away from them. They laid me with my feet facing the fire, my head pointing away. It was very uncomfortable. I looked up but all I could see was a canopy of darkness. Had the demons erased the stars? Josh was next, laid the same way, not quite straight across from me. Bucky would be next. Where was Ranger?

Suddenly a whirling dervish cloud of a dog attacked the head demon. He let out a yell. "Get that dog!"

"Yes, master."

The assistant demon soon had poor little Ranger trussed up in tape too. "Excellent," the head demon said. "Now we have the cardinal points all together."

I'd heard that head demon's voice before. I didn't have time to remember where before they moved me again, and I realized that the four of us were pointing in four different directions—north, south, east, and west. I didn't know which I was. Not that it mattered.

The head demon stood outside the circle, raised his arms, and intoned some kind of a chant. I couldn't understand a word of it. It didn't sound like words, just strange syllables, maybe another language? Igor knelt at his feet and held up a black case. The demon leaned down and opened it. Silver flashed from his hand. He held it so that it lay across both of his palms. The handle glittered with jewels in the firelight: rubies, sapphires, emeralds. Were those real? And then I realized what he was holding. A dagger! It looked real. It was a very fancy, probably very valuable dagger. What was he planning to do with it?

The demon's chanting rained down on us. He raised the dagger high above his head. Igor seemed to be in some sort of worshipful trance. They weren't paying attention to us. I lifted my head just enough to catch Josh's attention. He raised his head and looked back at me. Then I bent my knees and started rolling slowly away from the fire.

I willed Bucky to notice us but he seemed under a spell, his eyes fastened on the dagger. I was torn. I didn't want to leave him in the fire circle but if we got away, the demons would have to look for us and then he could get away too. It was a simple plan. I'll never know if it would have worked.

Chapter 15

I squirmed and rolled between two tombs. Josh was already out of sight. I wished he had come my way, but we were safer separated. The demons would have to split up to look for us. I looked back at Bucky one more time, willing him to see me, but his eyes were locked on the dagger.

The demon lowered the dagger. Igor stood and bowed to his master. They didn't even seem to notice we were gone. They concentrated on Bucky. They were going to kill him! Right in front of us, and there was nothing we could do.

I tried to scream through the tape, but only a muffled sort of squeal came out.

Bucky didn't move. Frantically I felt around behind me for something, the sharp edge of a tomb. I had to get free to save Bucky and Ranger. Where was Josh?

I skinned my wrist against something rough. Stone. I

rubbed the tape against it as fast and hard as I could, but nothing was happening. I rolled again and hit something solid. Another tomb? A wall? I willed myself to look away from the light of the fire, from what might be happening to Bucky and Ranger. My fingers were going numb. I forced them to feel behind me. Nothing but slick marble there. I rolled again and hit something hard and sharp. Metal. It had to be. A fence? I couldn't take the time to look.

My fingers were turning to stone as I tried to position my wrists to saw the tape on the metal. It must be a little wrought iron fence. There had to be a sharp edge on it. Back and forth I moved my wrists. I felt nothing from the tape down into my hands now. I could be sawing my own fingers off but I thought it was the tape. I hoped it was the tape. I hoped Josh was doing the same thing.

Was that a little split? Had the tape started to go? I worked my wrists faster. The tape seemed looser. The demons were both chanting now. They could be speaking words but it all ran together into monotone gibberish.

I risked my night vision for a glance at the fire circle. The firelight light seemed to change from the orange glow of flames to peach. Was the sun coming up? That had to be the cause. It must be later than we'd thought. I'd never seen such an eerie light, sort of pale chartreuse that darkened slowly.

Bucky lay like a stone in the circle with Ranger across from him. I tried to see if he was breathing. His eyes were fixed on something low on the ground and then I saw it too. The sun wasn't rising. The glow from the fire had died into embers as a greenish mist crept around the two demons. Slowly, hypnotically, it thickened around them, around the circle where we had lain arrayed like wheel spokes.

What was this? More of their mumbo jumbo?

I renewed my sawing but my arms were tiring. My muscles felt like they had turned to jelly and my hands were boulders at the ends of my wrists. Bucky whimpered, and Ranger made small sounds in his throat between a mew and a growl. The puppy didn't understand what was happening, and neither did I, except that I knew it was something bad and I had to get my hands loose. I took a deep breath, closed my eyes to that ghastly green mist, and pumped my arms behind me. Suddenly the tape popped loose. Both of my arms hit hard stone. It hurt a lot, but I didn't have time to feel it. I pulled the tape off my ankles and bolted up between the tombs, lunging for Bucky.

The weird chanting continued as the green mist darkened like emerald walls rising around the circle. I plunged through it at the same time that another shape came from the opposite direction.

Josh! He had got his hands free. He grabbed Bucky and I scooped up Ranger.

As we slid through the greenish mist I risked a look at the demons. Their faces were turned upward, their arms raised to the sky. I did not see the dagger. Was that a good sign?

"You did it, master," the assistant demon said with assistant demon modesty. "You have called forth the spirits of the dead to witness your power as you sacrifice these four beings."

"My power will increase fourfold with their deaths."

Terrific. A demon with an ego.

"I will be unstoppable."

Not if I can help it. We took off as he chanted another basketful of syllables. My teeth chattered with cold behind the tape as I ran, trying to keep up with Josh. Ranger had squirmed when I picked him up but he settled against me as if he realized he was being rescued.

"We are your disciples, O spirits!" the demons intoned behind us, their voices growing fainter.

Then I remembered where I had heard the voice before.

We ran through the city of the dead, silent now. I expected to hear the demons shout when they discovered we had escaped, but no sound followed us as the chanting faded. Our feet pounded the shell road as we reached the edge of the cemetery.

We crossed the street, clomped up on the porch and into the house. I slammed the door behind us and locked it. I put Ranger down and ran to check the backdoor, flicking lights on ahead of me. Still locked. Josh followed, and as I started to pull the tape off my mouth, he grabbed my wrist and shook his head. He got a dish towel out of the kitchen and used it to pull the tape off my mouth, then his. "Holy shit!" he said.

"You said it!"

"The tape has to have the fingerprints of one of those fiends on it."

"Unless they were wearing gloves." I tried to remember the demons' hands. They had been dark like the rest of them.

Josh removed Bucky's tape and laid each piece across the packing crate in the kitchen. Then he did the same for Ranger. The puppy yelped when the tape pulled his fur.

"Who *were* those guys?" Bucky whispered.

I didn't know what to tell him. "They're nutzos, Buckster. Some people get a little too into Halloween jokes."

"Some joke. Haha," he said, sitting on the floor with

Ranger in his lap, petting him and saying over and over, "It's okay, Ranger. You scared them off."

The house seemed so ordinary. So normal. I wanted to hug it. I sent Bucky to get ready for bed and went to find the phone, turning on lights as I passed through the rooms. I found Officer Parker's card and punched in the number. He answered right away. I identified myself and said I wanted to report a crime.

"What kind of crime, Courtney?"

"A kidnapping. Can you come to my house? And don't use the lights, okay?"

I had hardly put down the phone before the cruiser was in front of the house. Officer Parker bounded up on the porch.

I introduced him to Josh. "I don't know where to start," I said.

"Start with Bucky and the Halloween party," Josh suggested.

So I did. I told him the whole thing. He listened intently.

"We have the tapes that were on our mouths," I ended. "They're in the kitchen."

He made some calls and soon the cemetery filled with police, their vehicles and lights. Somebody collected the tapes.

"Any idea who the perps were?"

I looked at Josh. "Did the head demon sound like anybody you've heard before?"

"Yeah, but I can't remember who."

"I think the head demon was Dr. White."

Josh's eyebrows went up. "You're right!"

"That the writer been giving those talks around town?" Officer Parker looked at both of us.

"Yes. We heard him at school," I added.

"I heard him at the library and I talked to him once at the hotel," Josh said.

"What about Bucky?" Officer Parker asked. "We need to talk to him."

Bucky sat on his bed, holding Ranger. "I walked partway home with Jeff," he said. "We trick or treated. After Jeff left, something grabbed me. I didn't feel nothing, it was just black and sort of stuck to me," he explained. "I yelled but nobody heard me. They taped my hands and mouth and carried me for a while. Then they locked me in a dark place."

"I'm really sorry, Buckets, I should've been there to pick you up when the party was over."

"Why weren't you?" His eyes were round and serious. He didn't really understand that he had almost been a ritual sacrifice to Satan.

"I was telling fortunes at Jessica's party and lost track

of time," I said. "When we got here and you weren't home, we got Ranger to find you for us. He tracked you all the way to the shed."

"Wow! I knew he was the smartest dog in the world." Bucky lay down hugging Ranger, who snuggled closer.

"He's a great tracker," Josh said, looking at me over Bucky's head.

Officer Parker smiled at that. It was the only time he smiled that night.

Chapter 16

"Do you think those nutcases were really going to sacrifice us?" I asked Josh after Officer Parker had left.

"It sure seemed like it from where I was lying in that circle."

"What happened to them? They sort of disappeared in that foggy green stuff."

"I don't know. I think they thought they were being raised up to some higher spiritual world."

"Sounds pretty delusional to me. Do they have higher degrees in the Satanic world?"

He laughed. "I don't know. Probably. Otherwise, what would be in it for an American Satanist? They need to climb the Satanic ladder."

He could joke about it, but I wasn't over it yet. Maybe I never would be. I almost got my little brother sacrificed by a pair of would-be demons.

Josh was staring at the coffee table. "Jeez, Courtney,

it's real! What are you doing with a tombstone for a coffee table? I thought it was just a piece of stone."

"Mom found it in the backyard. She thought it would be cool to use it for a table."

"How did you pick it up?"

"I don't know. She did it when we were at school. Maybe Mr. Gower helped. Do you think they were just men pretending, or do they really believe they're demons?"

"How can you tell?" He laughed, but his laughter had a hollow sound.

"I'm not joking. I don't have a Demon's Manual that I can look it up in. Or an Idiot's Guide to Demonology."

"There probably are such things," Josh said. "People believe all sorts of screwy things, but *I* think Dr. White is a man pretending to be a demon. White may not even be his real name. I mean, come on, Gabriel White?"

"His real name could be Beelzebub Black. Do you think they were really going to sacrifice us?"

"Kill us, you mean?"

I shivered. I couldn't help myself. Josh slid an arm around me. I leaned back. His arm was warm, alive. It felt really really good. "Yeah. Were they really going to do it?"

"Guess we'll never know. But what about motive? If they were really going to kill us, were we sacrifices for

Satan? Or are they just murderers who like to dress it up? Or are they crazies who really believe all that stuff?"

"The world is full of weird people. If they weren't going to kill us, what did they do it for? And what was that green stuff?"

He shrugged. Then, "We need to look hard at motive. What did they hope to prove?"

I couldn't even imagine. "It had to be some kind of power trip," I said finally.

"Most motives usually are."

"At least the police believed us. I didn't think they would," I said. "Since it was Halloween and we're teens."

"Maybe they wouldn't have, but somebody else reported seeing a strange green light in the cemetery."

"Lucky for us."

"Yeah, real lucky."

"I forgot to tell them about little Lucky."

"I didn't. I have the pictures I took. I promised to take them to the station tomorrow."

"I was angry at you that day for treating it like a story for the paper. I'm sorry."

"It's okay. I might've thought the same thing in your shoes." He looked at his watch. "It's after one. If I sit here any longer, I'll fall sleep. I hate to leave you and Bucky here by yourselves."

"We'll be okay. The police are still patrolling. Anyway, I have a feeling those demons are long gone from Limbo Key."

We got up. At the door Josh pushed a hand through his hair. It flopped back over one eyebrow. "I need a haircut," he said.

"It looks great." His hair was adorable.

He opened the door. The dark came alive with a sudden scurrying.

"Jeez—Halloween rats?" I shuddered.

"Iguanas. Or maybe mice dressed up as rats. Don't worry about it. They can't open doors. Just keep the doors locked."

I walked to the edge of the porch with him. I hoped he would kiss me. And he did, a brief kiss. For a first time, it was a little disappointing.

"Let me see you lock the door," he said when I lingered on the step.

"Okay." I didn't move.

He didn't either. "I didn't know what to think when you ran out of the tent at the party. I thought you were mad at me over Jessica."

I started to say something, but he interrupted. "No, let me finish. Jessica and I had a few dates last year but we were never a couple. Anyway she liked a college guy who was down for the summer."

Was she nuts? Choosing a college guy who would

leave over Josh who was adorable and here year-round? "Jessica makes bad choices."

After a second, he laughed. "I would've caught up with you, but in your mad rush, you knocked over the table and the lantern. The tablecloth caught fire. I had to stop and help put it out."

"I didn't mean for that to happen. Was Jessica's mom mad?"

"No, she was just concerned about you."

"I'm sorry. I was only thinking about being late for Bucky. What happened to him is really all my fault."

"No, it wasn't. It was just bad luck that Bucky went home alone, but even if you'd been with him, they would have just taken both of you, like they did later. It's obvious they've been watching this house. They knew where to get Lucky."

"I guess you're right, but I still feel guilty."

"They've probably been doing stuff over there for a while, and you didn't notice. So they had to up the scare quotient."

"I hope that's all they were doing."

"I think it was. If they'd been serious about murder, I think they would have done it from the start. I'd better go." He kissed me again, longer this time, and it wasn't at all disappointing.

"Call me when you get home." I called as he loped off. I locked the door and left the porch light on for Mom.

I wanted a shower, but not tonight. All I needed was for Norman Bates to burst in. Or some other psycho.

Chapter 17

Something woke me. I glanced at the clock. 7:30. I flopped over to go back to sleep, but a bunch of green parrots squawked in the trees outside my window. They sure made a lot of noise for such small birds. By then I was fully awake. I got up and switched off my Goodwill lamp. No way was I sleeping in the dark last night, not even after Mom came home. We'd left the porch light on, so I switched it off as well.

I thought I'd sleep late after everything that happened yesterday. Was it only yesterday that I went to school dressed as Little Red Riding Hood? And told fortunes at Jessica's party? Both seemed like 1,000 years ago. After Josh's call I stayed awake, drifting in and out of sleep until Mom came home at around two. She was ready to fall into bed, too tired to talk. "I've talked enough tonight to last me a week," she'd said.

That was fine with me. I couldn't keep my eyes

open. "You didn't get married?" I couldn't resist saying, even in my sleepy state.

"Don't be—"

"An SA." I mumbled into my pillow. She laughed on her way to bed. Good for Mom. She'd developed a sense of humor.

I toasted a waffle and ate it with honey left from the motel breakfast bar on the trip down. We didn't have any syrup. Now that Mom was working, maybe our cuisine would improve.

Prompted by the sound of food being consumed in the kitchen, Ranger jumped off Bucky's bed and padded in. He looked hopefully at the fridge and the back door, torn between his needs. I shared a few bites of my waffle.

"Okay, little guy. You were a splendid dog last night. Let me put on some shorts."

We slipped quietly out the front door without waking Mom and Bucky.

Ranger went to his favorite tree and then his favorite corner of the yard. He was probably tired too, but I wanted his company while I looked for the site of the fire in the cemetery. We crossed the street. I remembered the general direction we'd taken last night. Ranger trotted along beside me.

In the morning light I realized that we had traveled

a haphazard circular path through the tombs in the oldest part of the cemetery. The tombs themselves were neglected, some with broken bricks, crumbling stucco, and sagging doors, but not the tombs that we were locked in. I recognized them because of the shiny new locks that somebody had recently put on solid old doors. I didn't try to go inside any. I'd already spent as much time in a tomb as I ever intended to, as long as I lived.

The fire circle had to be nearby. I didn't remember how far I had walked after I was taken out of the tomb. Ranger stopped suddenly to sniff something lying in the dewy grass. Josh's night goggles. I picked them up. He would be happy to have them back. Had the fire circle been this far? Then I remembered that I had walked some distance from Bucky's tomb before I fell into the open grave.

Was this the right direction? Suddenly Ranger bolted, and I followed. We careened around the corner of a tall imposing tomb and collided with somebody.

"Josh! Why didn't you tell me you were coming?" He looked good in the morning sun. He'd had a shower or maybe a swim, and his hair was still damp. He had on jean shorts and a navy T-shirt. I wished I'd had a shower or put on some lip gloss or at least combed my hair with more than three fingers.

"I woke up early this morning and couldn't go back to sleep. So I came over. I didn't want to wake you up."

"Same with me. Mom and Bucky are still dead to the world. Oops—I don't think I'll say that anymore."

"Yeah. Last night puts a new perspective on some things. What's that?" He looked at my hand.

I held out his goggles.

"Thanks. I was looking for them. They're my dad's."

We found the fire circle easily. "Shouldn't it be marked off with yellow tape or something?"

"I think that's only in case of murder," Josh said.

We were quiet, thinking how close we'd come to being murder victims last night. Maybe.

Josh cleared his throat. "I don't think the police think they intended to kill us."

"I'm surprised they believed us at all."

"Me too. Nobody believes things anymore around Halloween."

We examined the fire circle. It was just a ring like a kid might draw with a stick, but it gave me the creeps. "Let's go. There's nothing to see here."

"I stopped by the police station on the way over. The perps must have used gloves. No fingerprints showed up on the tape or the tomb doors. The police put out an APB on Dr. White and Igor. They got a description of the van and the tag number from the motel registration."

"So even if they're caught, it's only our word against theirs?"

Josh shrugged. "Guess we'll have to wait and see."

"Why did they do it?" I refused to believe that two adults could think they were really demons. There had to be another reason.

"I think they did it for publicity. We were meant to witness a Satanic ritual. They wanted us to escape and report it so it would make the papers. People would then buy Dr. White's book."

"That's disgusting."

"Yeah. But maybe not too farfetched. I've heard that some writers will do anything short of murder to sell their books. Anne Rice rode on top of a hearse or something to publicize one of her books."

"That's nothing like kidnapping."

"No, it isn't, but that was years ago. Publicity has gotten even crazier since then."

"Those horrible demons killed a puppy and kidnapped three people and another puppy for *publicity*? They scared us to death for *publicity*? That's sick. And worse than disgusting."

"And illegal if we could only prove it."

"What about that green fog? How did they make that stuff?"

"The cops found a bag with some kind of phosphorus stuff in it. They may have also had some kind of fog machine."

We headed back to the house. On the porch he said, "Want to go to breakfast somewhere in town?"

"Okay. Let me leave a note for Mom."

He waited on the porch while I took Ranger back to Bucky's room. He hopped back up on the bed and was asleep before I reached the door. I brushed my hair, spritzed on Vanilla Mist, and swiped on lip gloss.

Was this a date?

I left a note by the coffeepot in the kitchen where Mom would be sure to see it.

As we walked across the island, we passed porches populated by collapsed pumpkins with sagging grins like people who have taken out their false teeth. Bedraggled witches and drooping ghosts hung from trees and eaves. I sniffed the smoked pumpkin aroma. It was eau de day after Halloween.

Josh surprised me by going to the Seaside Inn. I would've showered if I'd known we were going to a classy place. I was glad I had spritzed and glossed. The dining room served a substantial breakfast buffet. We were both starved and went back for thirds.

When we couldn't eat anymore, Josh put down his coffee cup. "Did you have any bad dreams last night?"

"Well, there was this frog that kept trying to turn into a prince."

He smiled. It was a little lopsided, like he wasn't

wholly committed yet. His left eyebrow struggled and then it went up. He must have been practicing. "No, seriously."

"No, I didn't dream at all that I remember, but I did sleep with the light on. I haven't done that since I was eight."

"I haven't done it since I was five. I don't even remember if I had a light on last night. I was so tired. I fell into bed after I called you."

"I know one thing."

"What?"

"I don't think I'll ever get too much light."

"I know what you mean. It was black in that tomb I was in, but at least I was with Bucky. It must've been worse than a nightmare for you alone in that tomb."

"It *was* pretty bad."

"It's too much of a coincidence that Dr. White gives talks about Satanism and bingo, somebody paints satanic graffiti in the cemetery. Bucky's dog disappears. He's found in the cemetery, dead." He ticked them off on his fingers.

"It *could* have been some kind of accident."

"Mr. Gower said the screen was cut."

"Somebody could have tried to rob the house, Lucky got out, and then was killed somehow."

He shook his head. His hair stayed in place. "I think

he was supposed to be a ritual sacrifice, but we interrupted it."

I felt a little sick, and then I got mad. "I want to find
those demons."

He raised an eyebrow. "You're not scared of them?"

"Not in the daylight. Now that we know who and
what they are."

"Yeah. They go into a town, give free talks with
book signings, create enough vandalism to scare people
into buying more books. Then they move on to the next
town, but probably not one too close by."

"That's diabolical!"

"Exactly."

"What can we do?"

"For now, nothing."

I didn't like doing nothing. It was too much like
giving up.

Chapter 18

Bucky sat on the back porch sharing his breakfast Pop Tart with Ranger when I got home.

"Mom still sleeping?"

He nodded with his mouth full. He looked very serious.

"You okay?"

He shrugged and took another bite. Ranger pawed him and got another bite too.

"We sure had a Halloween adventure last night, didn't we?" I said chirpily, as if we had only gone to a party.

"Um hum."

"Ranger sure is a smart dog. He found Josh's goggles this morning."

Bucky finished the Pop Tart and threw his arms around the dog. Ranger climbed into his lap and licked crumbs and milk off Bucky's mouth. Bucky wouldn't even need a shower. The two were made for each other. I felt a pang about Lucky. He had been a sweet dog and didn't deserve what those demons did to him.

"There's just one thing that bothers me, Coco."

"What's that, Buckins?" I dreaded this.

"I don't have any trick or treats."

"What?"

"I lost my trick or treat bag last night."

I stared at him. He'd been kidnapped along with his dog, and the one thing that bothered him was losing his candy. "You must've dropped it."

"This morning Ranger and I looked where they picked me up, and I didn't see it."

"Maybe some other kid came along and found it."

He nodded. "That must be what happened. I wish I had some of that candy."

He didn't need any Halloween candy, but he deserved some. "We'll get some, Buckins. But first we have to go to the police station."

A scared look crept across his face. He buried it in Ranger's fur.

"You don't need to be scared, Bucky. Just tell what you remember, okay? Let's go."

"Ranger too?"

"Yes, Ranger can go too."

The police were gentle with Bucky. Chief Rodriguez gave him a police cap and a toy badge and one for

Ranger's collar. By the time they'd heard his story again, Bucky was ready to be a policeman himself, just like Officer Parker, and Ranger would be a tracker dog. I gave my official statement and signed it. Josh had given his earlier. They wanted Mom there, but I explained she was sleeping late after working last night. She could come down later.

We got a ride home in the police car. Bucky was thrilled when Officer Parker let him flash the lights just once.

That left Mom to tell. I could put it off for a while. Josh had asked us to go snorkeling.

"Can we take Ranger?" Bucky asked when I told him.

"I guess he deserves to go." I could tell that he and the pup were going to be inseparable from now on. We might have to set a place for Ranger at the table.

While Bucky changed to his swimsuit, I called Josh to tell him we were coming. I related what Bucky had said about losing his trick or treat bag.

"He's a great kid. He deserves some candy."

Mom got up then and regaled us with her triumphs. Her voice had recovered. "I have a gig for New Year's Eve at the hotel, and they want me to come on Thursday nights. With the beauty shops and the Bait Shack, it will be almost a full-time job!"

An almost full-time job was a lot for Mom.

"It was those cards I bought at the yard sale," she

went on. "You thought they were too expensive. Actually they were a bargain. Have you priced Tarot decks lately?"

"Um, no, not lately. How did all of this happen?"

"Remember, I told George's fortune and—"

"George?"

"Mr. Gower. Anyway I told his fortune, and he thought his customers at the Bait Shack would like to have fortunes told. From there one thing led to another. Coco, you can help me design a business card. Fortunes from Sabrina. Does that sound exotic? I'll need new costumes. I can't wear the same thing everywhere I go. I'll do mix and match. I'll look for a purple blouse tomorrow. Or do you think it should be gold? The jewelry might not show up as much with gold." She trailed away to the kitchen, her head filled with plans.

I felt proud of Mom. I didn't care if she was an artist or a fortune-teller. She was busy and so happy, so upbeat. I decided to put off telling her about last night. Besides, Bucky and I needed some time relaxing in the shallows of the Gulf of Mexico.

When we got to Josh's house, he had a small bag of candy for Bucky. "It was leftover from Halloween. We didn't have many trick or treaters last night."

The receipt was in the bag. I looked at it. The date was November 1. "Thanks, Josh," I mouthed over Bucky's head. What I really wanted to do was hug him, but I played it cool.

He shrugged and looked sheepish at getting caught being nice.

We floated above the turtle grass and coral castles, concentrating on that world, putting distance between us and last night.

Officer Parker was just leaving when we got home. "Officer Parker! Any news?"

"Um, no not yet. I just stopped by to get your mom's signature on these reports." He had pushed his sunglasses up and his blue eyes had a sort of dazed look. I knew that look.

"Are you married?" I asked him.

"Not now."

What did that mean?

Mom was dressed in green shorts and a lavender top. She looked happy. I hoped it was because of her career and not because Officer Parker had dropped by. George had some competition.

Bucky went to his room.

"We need to talk," Mom said.

"About what?"

"About last night."

"Didn't Officer Parker tell you what happened?"

"Yes, he did. That's not the point. I should've heard

it from you. Why didn't you tell me last night?"

"You were tired, and I was zonked."

She couldn't argue with that. "When I got up then."

"We were going snorkeling. I thought it was important for Bucky." She couldn't argue with that either.

"It was very embarrassing for a policeman to tell me what my daughter and son were doing last night."

"He didn't seem to think it was odd at all." He probably wasn't capable of thinking straight once he got a look at Mom. "In fact, he seemed to think you were just fine."

She smiled at that.

"Don't get—"

"I know. Married. Not planning to any time soon, but maybe someday. Before I'm fifty? Would that be okay?"

"Sure. As long as it's what you want and not something you think you need."

She gave me a look then.

"What?"

"Sometimes I think you're the mom, and I'm the daughter."

Sometimes I think so too, but for once I kept my mouth shut.

Chapter 19

Now that Halloween was over, it was time to get back to my career. On Monday, I scouted around for lockers and found three possibles. I noticed people had started spiffing them up. Had I started a fad? I passed a herd of freshmen girls carrying wallpaper, scissors, and tape and noted their direction. I was ahead on the column because I'd used Jessica's for Halloween and had Bitsy's ready for this week.

Word had got out that I was the fortune-teller at Jessica's party. People told me I'd been fabulous and at least two told me that their fortunes had already come true. I couldn't even remember what I'd told them. Even Carli seemed friendlier.

That's why I was shocked to see plastic poo on my lab seat again on Tuesday. I threw it into my purse and eyed the class. Nobody seemed to be looking at me except Josh. He didn't say anything, but what can you say about an offering of dog poo?

If nobody in this class was doing it, maybe it was somebody in the class before us, somebody who knew which was my station. But who?

After lab I ran into Jessica in the girls' rest room. She shot angry looks at me. "I want to talk to you."

We stared at each other until the others had left.

"Listen, Jessica, about Friday night—"

"I guess you want my mom to pay you. But I want to know one thing. How did you know the real fortune-teller wasn't coming?"

I thought about it and decided to tell her the truth. After all, I had almost burned down the tent. "I didn't. When you didn't invite me to the party, I decided to crash it. I tried to disguise myself, and your mom thought I was Madame Zizou."

She looked puzzled. "What do you mean? Why did you think I didn't invite you?"

"You didn't call or send an invitation or even tell me what time or where to go."

"I assumed you knew. When I said that everybody was invited I meant everyone. I'm sorry." She looked really contrite. I couldn't tell if she was acting.

"I'm the one who should apologize for crashing the party and impersonating Madame Zizou."

She grinned. "Actually that was pretty cool! I can't believe you had the nerve to do either one. I sure wouldn't. Anyway, everybody thought you were really hot at telling fortunes. How did you learn to do it?"

"It's a gift," I said mysteriously. "And now I predict that we're going to be late for class if we don't hurry."

"Why did you run away like that?" she asked as we walked down the hall.

"I was late to pick up my brother at his party."

She looked sideways at me. "Are you sure it wasn't something that happened with Josh?"

"Josh? No, what does he have to do with it?"

"Everybody saw him go in the tent and then you ran out and a minute later he took off after you. We thought something happened."

I laughed. "That's how rumors get started. Josh helped me look for my brother. The party was over when I got there, and Bucky was gone."

"Did you find him?"

"Yes—eventually."

"Oh."

She looked disappointed for a second. I wondered if she wanted Josh back. Or maybe she just wanted some juicy gossip. Too bad. I didn't tell her Josh stayed at my house until almost two and then kissed me good night, but I couldn't resist one little tidbit. "Bucky was okay about it, especially after I took him snorkeling with Josh Saturday."

Let that get around school. Maybe it would make the Bloggo column. Then I had a thought. Maybe it was Jessica doing the plastic poo thing.

I made it to algebra with the bell.

At my locker just before lunch Stacy said hi, even before I did.

"Oh hi. Listen, Stacy, do you know if Jessica has lab second period?"

"No, she has it fourth with me. Why?"

"Somebody left something behind after lab and I thought it might be Jessica's."

Stacy frowned. "Maria, Suzanne, Becky, Carli, and Jane have lab that period. I can't think of anybody else. Girls, I mean. Want me to ask around?"

"No, thanks, I'll take care of it." It *had* to be Carli Fuselier behind the plastic poo.

Next day I came prepared. I got a pass during second period and went to the lab. They were all hunched over the stations, working hard. Mr. Sherman was a lab demon. Over in the corner at my station sat Carli. On my seat.

During third period, I put the poo on my stool into my purse. After class I rummaged in my locker. At lunch I carried my tray to the popular table, a plastic bag over my arm. Jessica looked up. The table waited for her to give them the cue. "Oh hi, Courtney."

"Hi, Jessica." I put my tray down and pulled out the chair. Before I sat down though, I said, "Carli, I think this is for you. Somebody left it at your lab station." I handed her the bag.

She looked inside and said, "For me!" She pulled out a box that a clock might have come in. It was carefully wrapped in frilly paper and tied with a lacy pink bow. Carli Fuselier was printed in block letters on the tag.

"What's the occasion?" Jessica asked suspiciously.

Carli tore into the present. She lifted the lid off the box. Inside, nestled in yellow tissue paper, were all the plastic poos that she had deposited on my lab seat. The table erupted in laughter as I snapped Carli's picture with the disposable camera I had paid far too much for.

"What's this for?"

"Somebody must have thought you might run out of plastic poo," I said neutrally.

Carli's face turned red. "You'd better not put that in the paper!"

I raised an eyebrow. I had no intention of doing so, but let her stew for a while. I slid the camera in my purse and sat down across the table. I picked up my plastic fork and speared a broccoli floret. I had conquered my lunchroom terror and my tormentor in one fell swoop.

And maybe melted the last bit of that ice floe.

Chapter 20

Josh checked with the police every day. Dr. White and Igor hadn't turned up anywhere in Florida. "We don't know if they know the police are looking for them. They may just be lying low so they'll be reported missing. Then they'll show up with some cooked-up story and think they can reap publicity for it."

"Maybe they'll decide to come back because it's not working."

"We'll see. This is not over yet."

It seemed to be over with the dog poo on my seat though. Carli didn't speak to me but gave me a lot of dirty looks when she passed me in the hall or the lunchroom. That was okay with me. I didn't want to talk to her either. This wasn't going to be one of those situations where two enemies become best friends, though Jessica had turned out to be all right. Okay, not too bright to trade Josh in for a college guy, but that worked for me.

Stacy wanted to know if Josh and I were hooked up.

"Hooked up? What do you mean?"

"You've been spending a lot of time together. Are you an item?"

"Oh yes, we are definitely an item," I said. I didn't know what kind of item, but I didn't tell Stacy that.

The next day Josh said, "I heard what you did to Carli. How'd you know she was behind the plastic presents?"

"I played a hunch."

"What gave you the hunch?"

"I asked around and found out she sits at my lab station in second period. Then I saw her there myself."

"You were cool about the poo."

"What do you mean?"

"Well, a lot of girls would have squealed and made a big thing out of it."

I filed that away. Always keep cool in embarrassing situations.

"And then you turned the trick on her." He grinned.

After school on Friday, we sat on Josh's deck while Bucky and Ranger paddled in the shallows.

"I have a feeling something may happen today," he said. "According to the police, White's rooms are paid up through today and they'd left a lot of stuff there and might be back for it."

Josh and I both knew that the case might never come to court even if the perps were caught. It was our word against theirs. A good lawyer could work on the Halloween angle.

"Maybe we could wait for them at the Seaside."

"We should be more proactive than that."

"How?"

"Looking other places."

"Like where? Where haven't the police looked?" Dr. White's car was a white van with a Kansas license plate. No such vehicle had been found anywhere in the Keys.

"Think where they might go."

"You mean, think like a demon thinks?"

"Something like that."

"Works for me," I said. "Where do we start?"

"The last place they were seen is usually the place to start."

"That was in the fire circle."

"Yeah." Josh slumped in his deck chair.

"We've seen everything there is to see in the cemetery and the police have seen even more."

"Right. Nothing there."

A boat chugged by. I checked for Bucky. He and

Ranger were looking for shells on the edge of the shore, safely out of the boat's path.

The boat had a mast but its sails weren't up yet. It was chugging out of the channel to open water where it would hoist sail and then go wherever the wind took it. I looked at Josh. He looked at me.

"Boats!" we said at the same time.

Josh leaped up. "Let's go check the boat rentals."

"Buckets, put Ranger on the leash. We have to do some sleuthing."

"What's that? Can I help sleuth?"

"Sure you can," Josh said.

We walked down to the marina. Josh had brought along the photo from the article in the paper. None of the boat rental places had seen Dr. White. Ranger sniffed a lot of tires and peed on one that must have smelled the best. Or worst.

We sat on a bench under an orchid tree. Josh's mouth was a tight line, brows drawn almost together. I felt the same way, but I didn't want to get wrinkles.

"Maybe they rented a boat somewhere else. Or maybe they're holed up in a motel somewhere," Josh said.

"You mean they might have rooms in two different places?" This boggled my mind. We couldn't even afford one room at a time when we drove down here.

"They could be using the other one as a bolthole or something like that. Like spies and undercover ops."

"Oh boy, spies!" Bucky said. "What's an op?"

"Operator, Bucky. I thought the police checked all the motels and hotels in the Keys."

"Maybe they were disguised. You know, one of them could even be dressed as a woman. The police wouldn't be looking for a married couple."

"What about the other side of the Key? Over near the Bait Shack? Aren't there some boat rental places there?"

"You're right. Let's go back to my house and get bikes. It's a long way."

We fueled ourselves with food after all that sleuthing. Ranger too, but he only got bread crusts. "Sorry, fella. We ate our last can of dog food last night," Josh said.

I raised my eyebrows. "Teasing a dog?"

"Yeah. It's okay as long as he doesn't tease back."

Josh had helmets for all of us. I rode his mom's bike with Ranger in the basket. Josh put Bucky on the back of his. He put his camera in the basket. "Just in case," he said.

The speed limit was only 25 mph and most people had bikes or scooters so the traffic wasn't bad, especially on the back streets Josh took us on. I was a little wobbly at first. I hadn't ridden bikes much. I'd never had one of my own, but I soon got the hang of it.

We checked three boat rental places. Nobody had seen the demons, and no boats were unaccounted for. The guy at the last place remembered renting a boat to a man who didn't look like Dr. White, but a man who *did* look like him got in it before they left the dock. He couldn't remember the name that was used so he couldn't look it up, but he had a boat due today. "It's a little bit overdue," he said, squinting as he looked at the turquoise sea, smooth as a bedspread. "Shoulda been in this morning."

The man had the deepest tan I'd ever seen. It contrasted with his white hair, which made his skin look even darker. Hadn't he heard of skin cancer? Sunblock?

"We'll wait awhile and see if these are our guys," Josh said.

"I'm thirsty," Bucky said. "And—"

"I know. Hungry. Bucky, you just ate."

We walked over to the Bait Shack and Josh ordered us all lemonades. Mr. Gower wouldn't let him pay for them. "You didn't trick or treat at my house for Halloween. Consider them your treats."

I wondered if he knew he had competition in Officer Parker. I borrowed his phone and called Officer Parker to tell him about the boat rental. He didn't answer. I left a message on his voice mail. We went back to the boat rental dock to see if the demons had come in. The proprietor shook his head. "Ain't back yet, folks."

"Mind if we hang awhile in case they come?" Josh said.

"Naw."

We didn't have long to wait. I heard a buzzing sound and nudged Josh. The man heard it too. "Boat's coming, one'a mine, one I bin looking for," he said, shading his faded blue eyes.

"We better get out of sight," Josh whispered. We pulled Bucky and Ranger behind a clump of banana plants on the side of the building. We didn't want the demons to head back out if they saw us. I started taking pictures as soon as they were in range, peering through the lens as I leaned through the fronds.

"That's probably enough," Josh said. "You can get more when they're docked. Keep Ranger quiet, Bucky."

Bucky put his hand around Ranger's snout. The pup didn't like it. He was excited.

The boat roared in close, then the driver throttled back and the boat slid up to the dock, making waves that rocked the other boats in the slips.

"Showboater," Josh said under his breath.

A man got out and tied the line to the cleat on the dock. I looked through the lens.

"It's the demons," I whispered. I focused on Dr. White and clicked the shutter. "Gotcha!"

Chapter 21

I continued clicking the shutter, framing each shot of the demons getting their gear out of the boat. They had to pay for another day because they'd kept the boat out past check-in time. I snapped them doing that. Then as they reached the boathouse, they saw us. The two men stopped in their tracks. I've read about that a lot, but I've never seen it happen. Igor had one foot in the air to take the next step, and he just put it right down as if marching in place.

Dr. White backed up a step. "What is this, a delegation?"

"You could call it that," Josh said. "Where have you two been since Halloween night?"

"That is our business, not yours," Dr. White said.

"I think it's our business. Your little trick or treating made it our business," Josh said in a sharp voice.

"And the dog's business," I said meaningfully, looking White in the eye as I took more shots of him by himself and with Igor.

"Get out of our way," White snarled, and the two pushed past us.

We jumped on our bikes and pedaled to catch up.

The demons broke into a run. Their faces were red, and they were panting heavily as they reached a van parked behind a coin laundry. It was black with a Massachusetts plate. So they lied on their motel registration. Why was I not surprised? Igor slid the door back.

"Coco, it's my bag!" Bucky said, pointing at the backseat.

"What?" I looked in the van. A black plastic bag lay on the seat. "How do you know it's yours?"

"It's got a rip in the corner where Ranger's tooth snagged it. How did *he* get it?"

"Good question, Bucky." Where was Officer Parker?

"Don't be ridiculous," snapped Dr. White.

"They're going to get away," I said to Josh.

"They won't get far," he said.

Dr. White jumped into the passenger seat. "Drive, Leindorf!"

"They're getting away!" Bucky said. "Coco, stop them."

My trusting little brother thought I could stop demons in a huge van. I wanted to hug him.

In the distance a siren wailed. Too late.

And then to our shock, the van veered to the edge of the parking lot where it crashed into a palm. Officer Parker cornered his cruiser and skidded to a stop. He jumped out. "Stay back, kids," he shouted, pulling out his gun.

The van's doors opened at the same time. Dr. White rolled out one side, Leindorf the other. They rolled in the parking lot and screamed as they tore at their clothes.

Officer Parker put his gun away and cuffed Dr. White.

"Quick, get on the other side and stop Leindorf," I said.

Josh and I sped around the other side of the van to stop Leindorf, but he was too busy slapping at himself and rolling around to escape. The hot shells crunched underneath him. Officer Parker called for backup and then cuffed Leindorf. His shoulders shook.

"What's the matter?" I asked him. Was he crying?

He burst into laughter.

Josh and I looked at each other, puzzled. Then Josh doubled up, laughing.

"WHAT IS SO FUNNY?" I demanded.

"Oh Coco—" Josh laughed harder.

Officer Parker's backup arrived, and in a minute they were laughing too.

"S'not funny," Dr. White said in an attempt to be dignified while writhing on the shells.

"Help! Police!" Leindorf yelped.

I walked over to Dr. White to see what was going on. Bucky followed me. And then we both saw it and laughed ourselves, though not as uproariously as the police and Josh. Leindorf and Dr. White's clothes were peppered with ants. Very angry ants. It was an LOL moment.

"Oh, Buckins, you got the perps after all," I told him. He grinned back at me. Even Ranger seemed to be grinning.

"Serves you right, you bad guys!" Bucky said. I don't think he had ever talked back to an adult in his life.

Bucky's Halloween treats must have drawn every ant on this side of the Key. The ants swarmed all over the perps' clothes and chowed down on the fresh meat.

None of the policemen wanted the perps in their cruisers. Officer Parker finally sent one of them to a nearby store to buy some ant killer. He sprayed the perps liberally. After a while the demons stopped twitching and were hauled off to jail.

As it turned out, it didn't matter that there were no prints on the duct tape or any other evidence in the cemetery. Bucky's fingerprints were found all over his plastic bag of Halloween candy. Further tests showed that the bag had been in the van for several days, but none of Leindorf or Dr. White's prints were found on or in the bag. They said they did not know how the bag came to be in their van, that they had left the van behind the laundry while they were away because it was close to the boat rental. Leindorf said it wasn't locked; he had forgotten. Josh and I didn't remember hearing an opening click.

A woman, Mrs. Draco on Abaterra Key, swore that Dr. White and Leindorf were at a party at her house on Halloween night. The District Attorney declined to file charges on such flimsy evidence. The police told Dr. White and Leindorf not to come back to Limbo Key, but before that happened Officer Parker took Bucky and Ranger into the jail to show them the men in their cell behind bars. "A visual image is important to a kid his age. That's what he'll remember, not whether they were tried and convicted," he told us.

Bucky and Ranger both wore their police badges to the jail. They wore them all the time now except to bed.

The paper printed the story, slanting it to show the depths to which some authors would go to try to sell their books.

"Whatever doesn't kill you makes you stronger," Mom said after reading the article.

"Whatever doesn't kill you becomes copy," Josh said.

"That's pretty good. Did you make that up?" I said with admiration.

He grinned. "I wish."

Cemetery Street had turned out not to be a dead end for us after all. Things were going pretty good. The weekend after Halloween Mr. Gower came over with color samples for us to choose paint for the rooms. He planned to paint the entire interior of the house. I picked sea green, the color of the water when we snorkled with Josh. Bucky chose marine blue. And Mom picked sunny yellow for the kitchen, parrot green for the front room and hallway, and coral for her room. Mr. Gower painted the ceilings of both porches blue and the floors dark green. Our house on Cemetery Street blossomed in living color. We haven't decided on the outside wall color yet. Mom likes mauve, Bucky wants a red house, and I—well I don't know yet. Yellow for light? Josh wants lime. Even though he doesn't live in the house, he spends a lot of time in it.

Mr. Gower comes over a lot to discuss the house, but so far Mom is still single. I've noticed Officer Parker cruising Cemetery Street too. Maybe looking for perps. Maybe not.

I still sleep with a light on in my room, but now it's a nightlight, a glowing seashell that Josh gave me.

There's a home game Friday night. I'm saving the

date. I plan to casually mention to Josh that I'm not baby-sitting that night. Maybe he'll ask me to go with him. If he doesn't, I plan to say I'll see him there.

Bloggo's column: November 21

Who has the Prada of lockers? Will there be a locker winner at year's end? Ask the newsome twosome seen together at last week's game.